John felt like he was in a doll's house. Or a storybook cottage. Everything around him was bright and feminine. Not frilly. Feminine.

The love seat and chairs in the living room were covered in a white-and-blue floral print and there was a rolltop writing desk stacked with books that took up an entire wall. A candle was burning on a small table by the window.

He walked over to blow out the candle and saw an open Bible next to it. It obviously wasn't a decoration. Some of the verses had been highlighted with fluorescent pen, and there were bookmarks sticking out everywhere.

Fiona emerged from a room down the hall and caught him studying it.

"Part of the Kelly family legacy? A badge and a Bible?"

"No." She held his gaze. "But it will be."

KATHRYN SPRINGER

is a lifelong Wisconsin resident. Growing up in a "newspaper family," she spent long hours as a child plunking out stories on her mother's typewriter. She wrote her first "book" at the age of ten (which her mother still has!) and she hasn't stopped writing since then. Initially, her writing was a well-kept secret that only her family and few close friends knew about. Now, with her first book in print, the secret is out. Kathryn began writing inspirational romance because it allows her to combine her faith in God with her love of a happy ending.

TESTED BY FIRE

KATHRYN SPRINGER

Love Inspired

Published by Steeple Hill Books™

STEEPLE HILL BOOKS

Steeple
Hill®

ISBN 0-373-87276-3

TESTED BY FIRE

Copyright © 2004 by Kathryn Springer

This edition published by arrangement with Steeple Hill Books.

www.SteepleHill.com

Printed in U.S.A.

Do not fear, for I have redeemed you;
I have called you by name; you are mine!
When you pass through the waters,
I will be with you;
And through the rivers, they will not overflow you.
When you walk through the fire,
You will not be scorched,
Nor will the flame burn you.

—*Isaiah* 43:1-2

This book is dedicated to:

My parents, for your love, encouragement
and support through the years.

Cindy—you were the one who believed in this
book, in these characters and in me. Thank you for
listening, for asking questions, for allowing me to
alternately whine and squeal with joy (depending
on what was in the mail) and for all your prayers.
Love you, friend!

Grandpa Goldsmith—
thank you for the writing gene!

And especially to Pete, who gave me the freedom
and the time to pursue my dreams.
When I was tempted to quit, you said "Don't."
You are—and will always be—my hero.

Prologue

"**I** think I'll ride with you a while, John."

John Gabriel paused and looked at his chief in surprise. The man behind the desk chuckled and eased his bulky frame out of the chair with a fluidity that belied his size. "I've got two weeks until retirement...I thought I should say my goodbyes to the neighborhood."

John didn't believe him for a second. Seamus Kelly *was* the neighborhood. His great-grandfather had stepped off the boat with Irish soil still caked under his fingernails and nothing that separated him from the rest of the crowd but a burning desire to make a place for his family in America. He had found his niche working as a bobbie in the slum areas of New York City, and the badge became a legacy that was passed down through the generations. Everyone who worked at the department knew the story. The Kelly family was a legend in law enforcement. There was a cop sitting on every branch of the family tree.

"Do you want to drive?" John asked, dangling the squad car keys from one finger.

"Get away with you," Seamus said irritably, but the gleam in his eyes told John he was pleased with the question.

As they walked in companionable silence to the car, John realized he wasn't nervous around the man anymore. When he had been hired nine months earlier, he had secretly mocked the way the other officers revered their chief. After all, he was just a man. A man whose hair was thinning, whose middle was beginning to thicken and who sometimes forgot to schedule a night car on the weekend. In John's mind, a man who should pack the old thermos into the old lunch box and make a spot in the department for someone younger.

Yet for the amount of awe and respect Seamus Kelly commanded, his temper was also widely recognized. It erupted like a volcano with old Gaelic spewing forth like lava. John had seen it—and felt it—about a month after he was hired.

His training officer, Dennis Meyer, was unimaginative and rather lazy. John was hungry to learn everything about being a cop. He pumped Meyer for information, badgered him about the need for a progressive department and generally made a nuisance of himself, until the man snapped one day and went to Seamus. The next thing John knew, he was standing in front of the legendary Irishman himself.

"So," Seamus growled, his eyebrows almost meeting over his nose. "You and Meyer have a problem, eh? None of my men ever have a problem with Meyer, so that means *you* must be the problem."

"Officer Meyer is slow—he's getting old."

Seamus stood up and leaned over the desk. "Too

old?'' he snorted. "He's ten years younger than I am. You were still on the playground when Meyer was getting a medal for bravery.''

John stiffened.

"You had a chip on your shoulder when you got here and I thought Meyer would smooth it down a little. Fact is, I think you've given him one now.''

John almost smiled. Seamus saw it.

"You think turning one of my steadiest officers into a raving lunatic is going to get you a promotion, lad?'' Seamus's voice rose and several officers within hearing range suddenly melted into the woodwork.

"At least that proves he's still alive,'' John had retorted. "Sometimes I have to nudge him just to be sure.''

He couldn't believe he'd said that. Here came his walking papers for sure.

"So who does the *particular* John Gabriel want for his training officer?'' Seamus asked sarcastically.

"You.'' John said the first name that came to mind and realized it was the truth.

There was absolute silence. John waited for the bomb to drop. Then, Seamus Kelly started to laugh. It was more frightening than a downpour of Gaelic.

"Lad, you remind me of me,'' Seamus sputtered. "You just got yourself a new training officer.''

In an unprecedented move, the chief had ridden with him for four weeks and John had discovered during that time that the man's heart beat for two reasons— his family and law enforcement. Even after John's training was complete, Seamus still rode with him on occasion, bragging about his children and grandchildren. John always listened politely but unemotionally.

Family ties were something he had never experienced, although he'd finally taken a tentative step toward that mysterious phenomenon when he'd asked Kristen to marry him. When she'd said yes, he had experienced, for the first time, an inkling of what some would call hope. Once they said their vows, his life was going to change. Was going to be better...

"Swing by Sixty-Fourth," Seamus instructed now. "The owner of the Meritz Company called me yesterday and said some kids have been hanging around the warehouse."

So that was it. If Seamus told someone that something would get done, it would. He personally made sure of it. John turned the car around and it cruised stealthily down the street.

"I suppose they're throwing me a big retirement party," Seamus groused.

"No." John slid him a sideways glance. "We're throwing the party *after* you retire."

Seamus slapped his thigh and laughed. John allowed a smile to surface.

"Slow down." Seamus leaned forward suddenly. "I saw someone by the Dumpster."

John frowned. He hadn't seen anything. Still, he had witnessed enough in the past months to convince him of Seamus's instincts as a cop. He pulled over and Seamus was already opening the door.

"I'll check it out, Chief."

Seamus flashed him an impatient look. "I'm retiring, Gabriel, but I don't need a baby-sitter yet."

They approached the back of the warehouse on foot and John made sure he was ahead of his chief as they neared the building.

''Window's out.'' John made a slow turn with the beam of the flashlight. ''I'll call for backup.''

Suddenly, bodies erupted from the gaping hole in the glass, smoke trailing behind them. Three teenage boys were captured in the light, their eyes wide and full of panic.

''Our b-buddy—he's still in there,'' one of them stammered.

Seamus was disappearing through the hole before John could react. He called Dispatch, requesting both backup and the fire department, then turned toward the boys. They scattered in three different directions. John decided Seamus was more important. He broke the rest of the glass out with his flashlight and climbed through.

''Get out of here, Gabriel!'' Seamus was a dim shadow in the smoke-filled interior of the warehouse. ''It's not just a fire. Clear out!''

''He said there was someone else in here,'' John muttered, and then realized with sudden clarity that the only ones trapped in the building were he and Seamus.

There was an ominous popping sound and John instinctively threw himself at the older man. He felt his body connect with the chief's before heat enveloped him and his vision blurred. Something thudded into his arm, pushing him to the floor.

Sirens screamed in the distance. John pulled Seamus toward the window and saw hands reaching for them. Pain radiated through his body now and there was a gray haze around everything that was getting thicker.

I guess we'll both be retiring, John thought bleakly, before the heat totally consumed his thoughts.

Chapter One

Ten Years Later

The door opened at ten o'clock. A shaft of light escaped, stretching across the well-kept lawn and briefly illuminating a crescent-shaped flower bed, a pot of geraniums and a garden hose that hadn't been put away.

The dog appeared first, a German shepherd that practically exploded from the confines of the house. It turned a few circles and then attacked the hose. Seconds later, a person emerged. Blue jeans. White T-shirt. A glint of auburn hair.

"Come on, Colin."

The husky words were clearly audible from where he stood in the shadows.

He was going to strangle the chief. Finn Kelly was a woman. When John had gotten an urgent message from Seamus the day before about a family emergency, he had pressed into service an acquaintance who had two things—a private plane and an old girlfriend he wanted to look up—which had taken John from a hotel in Denver to Seamus's house in Miranda Station, Wisconsin. He'd assumed that Finn was one of the chief's many grandsons, and for some reason—which John didn't want to examine too closely—Seamus had failed to mention the family emergency was female. Only the tenuous thread of their past friendship had prevented John from leaving Miranda Station the minute he'd spotted Finn Kelly. When Seamus answered the door the next morning, John said the first words that summed up his feelings.

"Are you crazy?"

"Hello, John. It's good to see you again, too." Seamus smiled.

"Absolutely not."

"You saw Finn. I should have known you'd do your homework. When did you get into town?"

"You conveniently forgot to tell me that your family emergency was a woman. You just wasted your time."

"Fiona is my granddaughter, not just a woman. Would you like a glass of iced tea? Or maybe some coffee?"

"No, thank you," John growled. "I can't take time off from work to baby-sit some rookie cop."

"I talked to your boss yesterday," Seamus said. "He mentioned you haven't taken time off in about five years. I'd say you deserve a vacation."

John glared at him. "No."

Seamus lost some of his calm. "You are the only one I trust, John. Something is going on at the department. Maybe it has something to do with the fact she's the first female patrol officer. She won't talk about what's happening…she's distracted. I'm worried about her.''

"Maybe she's one Kelly who isn't cut out for a career in law enforcement," John said. "It could be she's bringing this on herself—"

"You meet her and decide," Seamus interrupted. "But I know my granddaughter."

"Just out of curiosity, how are you going to explain why I'm here?"

Seamus's eyes brightened. "You're an old friend, why wouldn't you come for a visit? And I happened to talk to Chief Larson at the P.D. He jumped at the chance to have you give his men some training on the latest techniques for handling Internet crimes."

John shoved his hand into the pocket of his jacket. "I'm not saying yes," he warned.

"Just say yes to dinner tonight," Seamus said. "Anne is making pot roast."

Fiona Kelly decided to walk home after work. She had half an hour before her grandparents expected her for dinner and she needed to clear her thoughts. Chief, as her grandfather was affectionately known even to members of his family, and her grandmother, Anne, invited her over for dinner at least twice a week.

After she had been hired by the police department in Miranda Station, she'd moved into a small house tucked in a grove of maples just beyond her grandparents' two-story brick home. It was tiny, made of fieldstone and wood, and had once been a guest house for the larger estate. As she got closer, she could hear Colin bark a greeting. Her spirits lifted slightly and she walked faster. His face appeared in the window, tongue lolling. The curtains moved vigorously, propelled by his wagging tail. She barely had the key in the lock and he was whining at the door.

"Colin, back!" She jumped to the side as he burst out.

Ignoring her, he ran around the yard and then veered back to attack the garden hose again.

"Colin, no!" She couldn't help it. She started laughing. "Leave the poor hose alone. It's dead. If you'd done that to those silly dummies at training camp, you wouldn't be out of a job," she scolded.

He blinked at her and trotted over, pushing his wedge-shaped face into her hand.

"Guilty conscience, hmm?" She rubbed his ear. "If you behave yourself you can come with me."

Shedding the uniform and the bullet-proof vest she wore for her shift was a welcome relief, and she changed into a white sundress sprinkled with blue flowers and pale green ivy. Stepping into a pair of leather sandals, she called Colin to her side and they headed over to the house.

As she walked into her grandparents' home through the open patio doors, she heard masculine voices. One belonged to Seamus, the other she didn't recognize. Her heart dropped suddenly and she pursed her lips. The previous month a man from the fire department had "unexpectedly" shown up right before dinner. As a teen, she had started praying for the man that God would someday bring into her life—the man she would eventually marry. It was difficult to explain to Seamus that the Lord didn't need any help from a matchmaking grandfather!

"Hi, Chief."

"Finn!"

As Seamus rose from the chair, Finn winced at the

stiffness in his movements. At seventy-five, her grandfather was finally beginning to show signs of his age.

"I see you brought that failure from the academy with you," he teased.

"He may have failed at the academy but he's succeeding as a pet." She reached up and kissed her grandfather's weathered cheek. "You'll hurt his feelings if you keep talking like that."

"Well, John, come and meet my granddaughter, Fiona, champion of the underdog."

The man who had been sitting with his back to her suddenly rose to his feet. Seamus's words dissolved in Finn's ears as she looked at the stranger in front of her. She was caught and held captive by two jewel-green eyes.

"Finn, this is John Gabriel."

The words pieced themselves together again, and Finn instinctively put out her hand, a gesture of politeness that the man ignored. Still trapped in his gaze, she frowned slightly.

"It is a pleasure to meet you, Fiona," he said formally.

Finn's hand remained empty and she glanced down. John Gabriel's arm was missing from the elbow down.

John watched the momentary confusion on her face but wasn't inclined to help her out. Then she astounded him by smiling.

"John Gabriel. You saved Chief's life, didn't you? You're practically family, then, and family members get hugs, not handshakes."

Before John could react, she stepped forward and embraced him easily. Over the top of her head, he saw

Seamus grin. He stiffened, but she had already let go of him, leaving a light, flowery fragrance behind.

''And call me Finn. Everyone does.''

''Finn, I thought I heard your voice. Snuck in through the patio, did you?'' Anne Kelly appeared in the doorway. ''Hi, Colin. Good dog.'' Colin thumped his tail in appreciation and Seamus snorted. ''Supper is ready.''

They filed into the dining room, the room that Anne Kelly saved for company, but there was nothing stuffy about the decor. The floors were hardwood that had mellowed over time and the curtains were a breezy muslin that welcomed the sunshine. The table was set for four.

John was still in shock from his introduction to Finn Kelly. The moonlight hadn't done her justice. Medium height and slender, she had delicate features framed by the pale auburn hair that had been passed down from the original Kellys. This young woman was a police officer? She looked like she wasn't old enough to hold a driver's license!

''Will you say grace, Finn?'' Anne asked.

Finn nodded and glanced at him. Her eyes were gray, ringed with indigo. The room suddenly felt very small. And he didn't even hear her prayer.

The following hour was spent in pleasant, but meaningless, conversation. Finn noticed that both Chief and John Gabriel carefully avoided bringing up old memories. She had been only thirteen years old when the accident happened. She vividly recalled visiting her grandfather in the hospital and hearing her family whisper about the young police officer who had used his body to shield Chief from the explosion. Her grandpa was all right, that was all that mattered in her way of thinking, but she knew that John Gabriel was a hero. She had heard his name mentioned occasionally over the years and knew that he and Chief still kept in touch, but she hadn't realized the extent of his sacrifice until now.

"What do you do, John?" Finn asked during a lull in the conversation. She felt the force of his gaze once again and it was unsettling. She had had a chance to covertly study him during dinner and decided he was an attractive man. A faint burn scar that ran from temple to chin didn't detract from the strong, clean lines of his face. His hair, the color of coffee with a splash of cream, touched the collar of his black polo shirt.

"I work for a private agency that investigates crime," he answered evenly.

Finn was silent for a moment, a nagging suspicion beginning to form. "What's the name of the agency?"

"I doubt you are familiar with it, Finn."

"Try me." She smiled sweetly.

"The Madison Agency."

Finn recognized the name immediately. "Another group of untouchables, right? The agency that solves crimes that are considered unsolvable. Wasn't it Madison that found that little girl who was kidnapped and taken to Pakistan last year?"

Seamus laughed, although it sounded a trifle forced. "My goodness, lass. Not too many people know about the Madison Agency."

"I read a lot," Finn said, winking at him. "Here, Gran, let me help you clear the table."

"Well," Seamus said earnestly, leaning forward after the women had gone into the other room, "just hang around here a little while and keep an eye on her. Tell me if all this is the product of an old man's imagination.''

John closed his eyes. What he saw in Finn Kelly was a woman who was too fragile for police work and didn't want to admit it. Maybe there was some kind of discrimination going on among a few of the men who couldn't stomach a female officer, but he doubted it was anything truly sinister.

"Chief." The title slipped out easily. "Don't you think that maybe—''

"Excuse me.'' Anne poked her head around the corner. "Seamus, Cory is on the phone. Shall I tell him you'll call him back?''

"Go ahead.'' John sighed, not wanting to deny Seamus a call from his son. "I won't run out the back door while you're gone.''

"See that you don't,'' Seamus muttered.

John had been alone for all of one minute when Finn came back into the room. How many women actually wore dresses for no occasion at all? He turned away and stared out the window.

"Mr. Gabriel? John—I know why you're here.''

Startled, he swung around and discovered she was inches away from him. "You do?''

Finn glanced at the door. "You found out about Chief's heart problems, didn't you.''

"His heart problems?'' John repeated slowly.

"He's had two minor attacks in the past six months,'' Finn murmured. "He doesn't like to complain, but I know he's in pain. Your visit will do him good. How long are you going to stay?''

John couldn't believe the words that came out of his mouth. "Probably just a week or so.''

Chapter Two

Finn got up early the next morning to go for a run before her shift started. Colin lifted his head and whined.

"I know it's early, but if I have to stay in shape, so do you." She turned on her CD player and hummed along with her favorite praise-and-worship band as the music pulsed through the house while she got dressed.

Dew brightened the grass and already the sun was warm with the promise of a beautiful day. She did some quick warm-up exercises on the porch and then broke into an easy run, with Colin loping along beside her.

Her grandparents' house was quiet, and she glanced up at the window of one of the rooms Anne reserved for company. The shade was still drawn. *John Gabriel.* Her heart gave a funny dip just at the thought of him and it surprised her so much that she stumbled. Grinning, she saw Colin looking up at her.

"Crack in the sidewalk." She laughed.

The man was a mystery. He must have been close

to her age when the explosion cost him his arm and his career as an officer. Now he worked with the Madison Agency. She had never met anyone affiliated with it before. Its headquarters were in Chicago, where part of the Kelly family had settled in the 1920s. The agency was low-key, the average person wouldn't even be aware it existed, yet it had a reputation for excellence in cutting-edge investigative techniques. Some said it was a wild card—a maverick agency that walked on the edge of the law to solve crimes. Somehow she sensed that Madison and John Gabriel were a good fit.

As she jogged around the side of the house, Finn saw the man she had just been thinking about, standing on her porch.

"Good morning, John." She slowed down and walked the few yards that separated them, hooking an errant strand of hair behind her ear. She tried to ignore the strange fluttering in her stomach at the sight of him.

"Finn." He leaned down and scratched a spot behind Colin's ear. "Anne sent me over to tell you she baked cinnamon rolls this morning."

"I have to be at work in an hour but I suppose I can make time for that," Finn said. Her heart was still pounding, but now she wasn't sure if it was from her run.

"I'll tell her," said John.

Finn disappeared into the house, and John watched Colin rolling in the grass.

"Sit!"

Colin leaped to his feet, then sat down and looked at him questioningly.

John smiled. "So, you haven't forgotten all of your training, have you, boy." He knelt beside the dog and glanced toward the house to make sure Finn wasn't in

view. "Well, we're going to start working together."
He pulled a piece of cinnamon roll out of his pocket
and fed it to the shepherd. "Just don't tell your com-
manding officer, okay?"

Anne had been bustling around the kitchen, and as
soon as John told her that Finn was coming over, she
poured another cup of coffee and brought it to the
patio.

"Good morning."

At the sound of the smoky voice, John looked up
and almost groaned. Finn was wearing a light-blue uniform, but instead of looking like a figure of authority,
she resembled a high school kid dressed up for career
day. Her hair was neatly braided and pinned up in the
back. She probably thought it looked more professional, but all it did was enhance the delicate planes of
her face—the luminous gray eyes and smattering of
freckles across her nose. No wonder some of the officers might be having a difficult time accepting her as
an equal.

"Good morning." Seamus smiled at her affectionately. "You got your run in this morning?"

"Most of it." Finn took a sip of coffee and closed
her eyes briefly in appreciation. "Mmm. This hits the
spot. I've got to watch for Carl. He's picking me up in
about twenty minutes."

John didn't think she sounded like someone who
dreaded going to work. She seemed relaxed. Maybe the
change in mood that Seamus detected was her concern
about his health, and nothing related to her job at all.

"Are you free for supper tonight, Finn?" Anne
asked.

John felt Finn's eyes on him. "No, I think I'll go to

the range after work this afternoon. Do you want to come along?'' She directed the question at him.

''Finn.'' Anne frowned at her, but Finn didn't acknowledge the warning.

''Were you right-or left-handed before the accident?''

''Right.'' He knew his voice sounded tight. What did she think she was doing?

''I'm assuming as a Madison agent that you still shoot.''

''Yes.''

''I'm probably better than you.'' Finn grinned mischievously. ''Want to find out?''

''Fiona Isobeale Kelly!'' Seamus blustered, but John held up his hand.

''It's all right, Chief. What man can resist a challenge like that?''

''I'm done at three,'' Finn said. ''I'm sure you can use Chief's gun if you didn't bring yours along. Otherwise I have an extra.'' A car horn sounded from outside. ''Carl's here. I'll see you all later.'' She filched another cinnamon roll and slipped out the door.

They sat in silence for a few minutes, then Anne forced a smile. ''I've got some laundry to get on the line. Help yourselves to more coffee if you'd like.''

''Seamus, did you get Finn the job here?'' John asked bluntly when they were alone.

''She scored highest on the civil service test and passed every requirement they had,'' Seamus said.

''That's not what I asked, but thank you for answering the question anyway.'' John stood up and walked to the window. The squad car was pulling away. ''She looks about sixteen, Chief. Did you think that securing a job for her at a department that's got any anti-female sentiment was a good idea?''

''You know as well as I do that being a good cop starts here.'' Seamus thumped his chest. ''She's bright and has integrity and compassion.''

''Then she should have joined the Girl Scouts,'' John shot back.

''Finn got the job on her own merit,'' Seamus insisted. ''All I did was talk to Chief Larson when she applied for the job. He said that he'd put in a good word for her with the Police and Fire Commission. There's been some pressure to start hiring female officers.'' Seamus saw the doubt on the younger man's face. ''She can do this, John. Everything seemed fine when she started at the department. Then, about two months ago, things changed. I can't put my finger on it. It's just a hunch, but something's going on. She won't confide in me or Anne.'' He looked like the admission stung.

''So maybe she can do the job—but does she want to?'' John asked. ''That's the million-dollar question.''

''There was another fire last night,'' Carl Davis told Finn on the way to the department.

''Where was it this time?''

''Just a shed behind the hardware store.'' Carl adjusted the rearview mirror. ''Someone reported it before it did too much damage.''

Finn shook her head. ''That makes two this month. The first one was in a Dumpster. Now it's a building?''

''School's out and kids are bored.''

''When I was bored I went swimming or played basketball,'' Finn said.

''Yeah, well, you probably had a pool.''

"Just a small one."

She liked Carl. He was in his early forties, with almost twenty years of experience on patrol. He'd begun as her training officer and still kept a close eye on her. Early on, he had told her she could confide in him if she had any trouble being accepted by the rest of the officers. She had gotten to know his wife, Sherilynn, and had taken them up on several of their dinner invitations since she'd been hired.

They walked into the department and the dispatcher, Gil Patterson, shook his finger at her. "There you are, Kelly!"

"What's wrong?"

"What's wrong? You had court a half an hour ago, that's what's wrong." Gil rolled his eyes.

"Why wasn't I told?"

"I put the notice in your box last week myself," Gil said defensively. "It was Lessing. They had to let him go because you weren't there as the arresting officer to testify."

Finn felt sick. Lessing. "I didn't get the notice."

"Chief wants to see you." Gil wouldn't look at her now. "He's in his office."

Finn had arrested Jerome Lessing for domestic abuse the week before, after a neighbor called to report sounds of a woman screaming. She had witnessed firsthand the bruises on Bonnie Lessing's face and arms when she'd arrived at the scene. And now the abuser had walked away without so much as a slap on the wrist.

Chief Larson was sipping coffee when Finn stepped into his office.

"Kelly." He indicated the chair on the opposite side of the mammoth oak desk. "Have a seat." He put down his cup. "Lessing's at Marie's Café this morning eating their dollar-ninety-nine breakfast special—one egg, scrambled, toast with jelly and home fries. Must not care about his cholesterol level."

"I didn't get the notice."

"I already talked to Gil. He remembers putting it in your box," Chief Larson said.

"Someone took it out." There, she'd said it.

Larson stared at her in disbelief. "Someone took it?" he repeated. "You mean deliberately? Are you saying there is some sort of...plot...against you?"

"Not a plot," Finn said in frustration. "It's just that little things have been happening lately."

"It doesn't wash, Kelly. You started out fine. The other officers have accepted you." He looked disappointed. "I can't let you blame your negligence on someone else. Has anyone in this department said they don't want you here? Discriminated against you?"

"No."

"You've got two months left on your probation," Larson said gruffly. "Let's see some focus, Finn."

"Yes, sir."

She walked out of the office and found Carl waiting for her.

"How did it go?"

"He gave me a promotion," Finn said, but the joke fell flat.

"Seriously."

"Seriously? I'm in serious danger of losing my job if I don't focus."

Carl frowned. "I'll talk to the chief."

"No, please don't, Carl. I can do this."

"Here, you can start with some follow-ups, then."

He grinned and pushed a stack of paperwork into her hands.

The well-kept, petunia-studded city of Miranda Station boasted a population of ten thousand people, but Finn definitely earned her salary during the day. By the time she came off her shift, she was tired. The next officer on duty dropped her off at home and she walked up the sidewalk, looking forward to having a cool shower and a change of clothes. She remembered that she had asked John Gabriel to go to the range with her. Well, maybe *asked* wasn't the right word. She had challenged him. And he hadn't disappointed her.

She peeled off her uniform shirt and bullet-proof vest and immediately felt ten pounds lighter. The shower revived her body but not her spirits. Finn knew she hadn't gotten a court notice in her box. Was Gil the person who was against her working there? Dispatch handled all the reports, and he had complained several times that hers weren't accurate when he checked her numbers against the computer.

She had just changed into blue jeans and a T-shirt when she heard a knock. Her hair was still damp from the shower and she fluffed it with her fingers as she went to answer the door.

''Come in.'' Finn stepped back as John's tall frame filled the narrow foyer. ''I'll be right back.''

John felt like he was in a doll's house. Or a storybook cottage. Everything around him was bright and feminine. Not frilly. Feminine. The love seat and chairs in the living room were covered in a white-and-blue print and a rolltop writing desk stacked with books took up an entire wall. The hardwood floors were scattered with bright rag rugs, and an oval-shaped breakfast nook held a small oak table scattered with more books. Along the top of the cupboards was a variety of ceramic teapots. Even though she had only been home from work for half an hour, a candle was burning on a small table by the window.

He walked over to blow out the candle and saw an open Bible next to it. It obviously wasn't a decoration. Some of the verses had been highlighted with a fluorescent pen and bookmarks stuck out everywhere.

Finn emerged from a room down the hall and caught him studying it.

"Part of the Kelly family legacy? A badge and a Bible?"

"No." She held his gaze. "But it will be."

Chapter Three

"Some people use both of them to hide behind," John said, watching her expression to gauge her reaction.

"Some people know the difference between finding shelter and hiding. Do you?" Finn tossed something at him and instinctively he reached out and caught it. A key ring. "You can drive."

They walked in silence to the garage, where two cars were parked side by side. One was a dark-blue import, compact and conservative. The other, a hunter-green Jeep Cherokee. Automatically he walked over to the import—and heard Finn chuckle.

"That's Chief's car."

He raised his eyebrows and regarded her thoughtfully. "My mistake."

Finn slid into the passenger side of the vehicle and waited. Just as she suspected, John was at home behind the wheel of a car. He turned the key and immediately they were drowned in music as the radio came to life.

Finn nudged the volume button down. "Sorry."

"A Jeep and loud music," John muttered. "Are you sure you're not sixteen?"

She didn't take offense. "The Jeep was a graduation present from my parents when I got my Criminal Justice degree last year. And the music, well, some things you just never outgrow."

"Right." John eased the Jeep out of the driveway. "Where do I go?"

"That way." Finn pointed left. "The range is about three miles from here." Finn leaned back and closed her eyes, feeling the tension from the day start to uncurl inside of her.

"Long day?"

She didn't answer right away. *The court notice...*

"Well, there was that dog I had to chase for three blocks and the little old lady who wouldn't let me help her cross the street. Other than that—" Her voice broke off and her eyes snapped open because she heard a strange sound. John Gabriel was laughing. Granted, it sounded a little rusty, but it was laughter.

"The hazards of the job." He turned a smile on her that transformed his austere features and turned her insides into jelly.

Finn swallowed. "You should do that more often."

"What?"

"Smile. Laugh. You know—try a variety of facial expressions."

"Very funny." John turned his attention back to the road. "Where do we turn?"

"Back there about a quarter of a mile." She realized that they had passed the road. It was his fault for laughing and causing her to forget her navigational responsibilities.

He turned the Jeep around and headed back. "Do you come here a lot?"

"Two or three times a week," Finn said absently.

"Is that required by your department?"

"No. We come out as a department about every six months. Dad says I should practice more than that. Most officers never fire their weapons, but you need to be accurate if you ever have to."

The range was an open field with oak trees bordering the perimeter like silent sentinels. No one was there, and Finn was glad. Now that she had bullied John Gabriel into this, she was having doubts.

"Okay, Annie Oakley." His voice was so near it startled her. "You first."

He set up the targets while Finn pushed the clip into her handgun and put on ear protection to muffle the sound.

John watched as Finn stepped up to the line. Everything about her stance and posture was correct. Correct but wooden. For someone who came to the range two or three times a week, she seemed almost uncomfortable with a gun in her hand. The first few shots were close to the center. Then, something happened. Her concentration dissolved. The next few shots were way off. When she finished, her hand fell to her side and her head dipped slightly.

"Hey, where did you go?" he asked sharply, watching as Finn's head snapped up again and she smiled sheepishly.

"Daydreaming, I guess."

"Daydreaming?" He repeated the word in disbelief. "If that target decided to shoot back, I'd be picking you up off the grass."

"Your turn." Finn stepped back and looked away

from him. She couldn't explain what had just happened, other than the fact that Jerome Lessing's face had suddenly loomed in her thoughts. He was free and it was her fault. *Or was it?*

Gunfire brought her back to reality, and she watched as John pounded six bullets directly into the center of the target.

John glanced at her, expecting to see amazement or disbelief or any of the other expressions that people had when a one-armed man actually achieved something. Instead, she was looking at him proudly. Knowingly. The admiration on her face shook him to the core, momentarily shattering the wall he had so painstakingly built over the years. Then he knew. When she had invited him to come to the range—when she had casually tossed her car keys to him—she was telling him she saw a man. Not a one-armed man. Not a man with a scar that disfigured part of his face, and had, as some people assumed, seared his brain in the process. But a man.

No one had given him a gift like that in years. No one except his colleagues at the Madison Agency, who had stopped treating him with kid gloves just a few months after he started working there. It hadn't taken Finn that long. They had known each other less than twenty-four hours.

He wondered why he found the discovery so unsettling.

"Do you mind living so close to your grandparents?" John asked later as they headed back to the city limits. Now she was behind the wheel, which gave John a chance to study her. He couldn't put his finger on it, but there was some emotion still lingering in her eyes that he'd noticed when they'd been at the range.

"No." Finn shook her head. "When I got hired here, they wanted me to live with them, but I talked Gran into letting me fix up the stone house. I lived with my folks the whole time I went to college and I wanted a little space. They understood, and I don't mind living in their backyard. Especially now that Chief is having some health problems."

"I was surprised to see they had such a huge house to take care of." John remembered his first glimpse of the sprawling two-story brick home as the taxi delivered him the night he arrived.

"When Chief retired, he and Gran handpicked Miranda Station. They were tired of city living and wanted a place that everyone could come home to. It's still close enough to Chicago for impromptu family get-togethers. That's why he had the pool put in, too, for all my relatives to enjoy when they come for a visit. I don't think Chief has ever put his big toe in the water."

The stately brick home they were discussing came into view and Finn eased the car into the garage. There was a vacant spot where the other car had been parked earlier.

"Looks like they went out," Finn said.

"Your powers of observation are amazing, Officer Kelly," John murmured.

She looked at him in mock surprise. "A sense of humor, Agent Gabriel? Be careful, I may think you *are* human."

A strange expression suddenly came over his face, igniting some unidentified emotion in his eyes.

"Oh, I'm human, Finn," he said quietly.

Finn tried to smile but found she couldn't. A shiver of awareness rippled through her. She could hear Colin barking in the background, but everything else around her had gotten fuzzy. *What's happening here, Lord? Is John someone You've brought into my life for a reason...or am I supposed to run as fast as I can in the other direction?*

"I think this is the night Chief and Gran play Scrabble with the Silvermans. I was thinking about grilling some burgers." She offered the invitation as quickly as it popped into her mind. "Are you hungry?"

John hesitated. He reminded himself that he didn't want to be here. He didn't want to get involved with Finn Kelly on any level, but he had made a promise to Seamus.

"Never mind." She quickly picked up on his reluctance. "I just thought..."

The evening sun filtered through the trees and caught the fire in her hair as she pushed it away from her face in the unconscious gesture he was becoming familiar with. Remembering her lack of concentration at the range, he decided to push a little deeper to see if he could discover what was bothering her. Most likely she had been thinking about a boyfriend. Still, the way she seemed to disappear for a few minutes there worried him. A cop couldn't afford to do that on duty. The stakes were too high.

"Sure. A burger sounds great."

Her easy smile surfaced again, with no sign that she was aware of the tension that had just crackled around them minutes before. He didn't even want to go there. The connection he felt with her was undeniable and unexpected. And unwelcome. In the first place, he was ten years older than Finn in age and one hundred years older than her in experience. *Keep telling yourself that, Gabriel.* He followed her into the house.

"What do you want to do?" she asked him.

"Let's say I'm better at the outdoor range than at the indoor kind," he admitted.

Finn studied him thoughtfully. "I'll bet it's hard to butter bread."

Was she always this refreshingly honest? "I eat out a lot."

"You can flip the burgers, then."

"Can't I just watch television while you make supper?"

"Very funny."

He raised his eyebrows. "Am I laughing?"

"No, I think you fulfilled your quota of laughter already. Once a day?"

He had to actually *try* not to smile. She handed him a metal spatula, rummaged into the refrigerator for the pre-shaped hamburger patties and tucked a canister of seasoning salt under her elbow. "The grill is out the back door."

The back of Finn's house was a surprise. A flagstone patio fanned out in a V-shape, bordered by tall, colorful flowers and terra-cotta pots lined up on an old, weathered bench. The pots were home to a variety of vegetable plants. A faded quilt was folded neatly on a wicker chair and a grapevine wreath decorated an antique light pole.

Within minutes, she had the grill started.

"I'll be right back." Finn disappeared into the house and returned a few moments later with two glasses of iced tea.

"Thanks." He started to take a drink and paused. "There's something floating in it."

"It's a violet." She inspected the coals and frowned.

"You want me to drink a flower?"

"Not necessarily. But it won't hurt you if you do. Violets are edible," she explained patiently. "I put them in the tea because they're…"

"Go on. This is fascinating."

He had that detached, intimidating look on his face again, and Finn suddenly balked at telling him why she had dropped two violets into his iced tea. It had been done out of habit and now she was backed into a corner, having to explain.

"Pretty." She busied herself by salting the meat.

"Pretty." He repeated the word as if he'd never heard it before.

"Yes, pretty." She straightened and suddenly wished she hadn't done it in the first place. "Because they look pretty in the iced tea. Don't you think so?"

He studied the glass again, and she finally clucked her tongue.

"John, it's not a piece of evidence, it's a glass of iced tea. Just drink it."

He did, so cautiously that she had to chuckle, her initial defensiveness melting away.

John glanced at her and was relieved. If she was angry with him, it would be more difficult to find out if anything was going on at the Miranda Station P.D. He figured the sooner he found out what was wrong, the quicker he could get back to the Madison Agency and bury himself in the latest investigation he was working on. Seamus had been right about his not taking vacation time. He didn't want time to relax or be idle.

That gave him too much time to think about things better left alone.

Finn set plates on the small bistro-style table by the grill and put the food out. "Do you mind if I pray?"

John shook his head and waited to see if he recognized the table prayer, so he could stumble along.

"Lord, thank You for this day. For the things You've allowed in our lives—the challenges and the joys. Thank You for John and his willingness to take time from his busy schedule to spend some time with Chief…and thank You for the food you've provided. Amen."

For a split second, he was frozen in place as her prayer sunk in. *For the things You've allowed in our lives.*

There'd been more challenges than joy in his life and he'd never stopped to consider that maybe God was there during both. Well, if He had been there, He'd been standing on the sidelines watching. Distant and unavailable.

Chapter Four

When John walked into the chief's house after supper with Finn, the telephone was ringing.

"Kelly residence," he said.

There was a slight pause. "John?"

"Neil?"

"It is you!" The man on the other end of the line chuckled. "It took a while for Bradel to tell me where you were. He said some dirty word like vacation, but I figured it must be some kind of cover."

"I'm visiting a friend for a few days."

"Business or pleasure?" Neil Avery's voice was full of curiosity, and John sighed.

"Business of sorts," he admitted. "Did Bradel give you this number?"

"Only after being offered a bribe of two dozen homemade chocolate chip cookies," Neil said. "He drives a hard bargain."

There was a click and some static, then a third voice joined in.

"Neil? Is that John? Oh, you found him!"

"Hello, Diane."

"Hello, yourself. I've been worried sick about you, taking off like that without telling anyone."

"You sound like a mother hen. I told my *boss* I was leaving. I didn't realize I had to check in with the rest of the crew."

"Well, you do," Diane Avery sniffed.

"John isn't on vacation," Neil said. "It sounds like business as usual."

"Is she pretty?" Diane responded teasingly.

"Actually, yes." John couldn't resist.

Silence reigned for a moment, then both Neil and Diane started talking at once. John winced and held the phone away from his ear.

"Tell us everything," Diane demanded.

"Not a chance."

"Just one thing," Diane begged.

"You'd like her," John said slowly, knowing that Diane wasn't going to let him off the hook easily.

There was a sudden gasp of understanding. "She's a believer, isn't she."

"Let's say you seem to have some common ground," John said. "Now, don't you have some cookies to bake, you traitor?"

"Yes, I do," she said cheerfully, then added, in a stage whisper, "Find out more, Neil!" A click sounded as she hung up.

"Your wife never gives up."

"She should have been the investigator," Neil agreed. "When are you coming back?"

"I'm not sure," John said. "I didn't give Bradel a specific date. I have some time off and I'll come back when everything here is taken care of."

"Diane's almost due, you know," Neil reminded

him. "She wants your face pressed against the glass in the maternity ward, cooing with the rest of the Avery fan club."

"I'll be back by then." John heard the sound of a car door slam, signaling Chief's and Anne's return. "I'll call you soon."

"John?" Neil caught him just as he was about to put the receiver down.

"What?"

"*Is* she a believer?"

"Goodbye, Neil."

Later that night during her run, Finn took advantage of the quiet streets and let Colin off his leash. He trotted happily along beside her.

"What's with you lately?" She couldn't explain the dog's sudden obedience. It was as if he'd grown up overnight. "Did someone slip something into your food?"

As she ran, Finn replayed the evening with John. She was surprised that he had accepted her offer to join her for supper. *You read too many books when you were a kid,* she scolded herself. All those stories about Sir Lancelot and knights and heroes. When she was thirteen and Seamus had been injured in the explosion, she'd been reading about the Middle Ages. Secretly, she had thought of John Gabriel as "the white knight" because of his heroism.

"He's more like the black knight," she murmured out loud. He had built a fortress around himself. It was easy to discern that cynicism was his sword, bitterness his shield. Maybe the accident had caused him to put up the barriers she saw.

"I can't figure him out, Colin."

Colin growled.

The sound was so unexpected that she stumbled to a stop.

"Hey," a voice drawled from the bushes. "It's that lady cop."

"She ain't on duty now, though."

There were some snickers and muttered comments. Finn decided to keep going and ignore them—until the two young men stepped out of the shadows and blocked her path. One held a cigarette loosely in his hand. She recognized him immediately. Ricky Calhoun. His dad owned the largest construction company in Miranda Station. Ricky was a few years younger than she, but he worked for his dad only when he needed extra cash, which wasn't often. He drove his dad's car and generally hung around town doing nothing. He seemed to be making a career out of being the only son of a wealthy businessman.

"Hello, Ricky," Finn said evenly.

His companion thumped him on the back and laughed. "She knows your name, Ricky! Have you ridden in the *back* of the squad car or something?"

Ricky grinned and flicked the cigarette into the street, the end still glowing like a single red eye. "I'm a good boy, Marty."

"Excuse me." Finn tried to move past them, but Ricky stepped in front of her again.

Colin suddenly slipped alongside them like a shadow and planted himself next to Finn. She reached down, feeling comforted by his presence. "Stay, Colin," she said, hoping the dog would actually listen to her.

Ricky glanced down at the shepherd, whose lips had curled back to expose a set of intimidating teeth. He took a wary step away from her.

"See you later, *Officer*."

Finn nodded briefly and started to run again, aware of the fact they were watching her. Marty apparently found something else amusing, because his laughter echoed down the street behind her.

"You must be a good judge of character, Colin," she said. "And by the way, thanks for your support."

Colin dashed into a row of bushes and emerged half a block away. When she whistled, he ignored her.

"At least your timing is good." She shook her head.

A half an hour later, she jogged back up her grandparents' driveway. All the lights were out except for the guestroom upstairs.

She had been so tempted to confide in John about her problems at the department. The small changes in her reports, the missing court notice. Would he accuse her of not concentrating? Of not being able to handle the job? She had no proof that someone was undermining her work.

Lord, You see what's going on...show me what to do.

She got ready for bed and curled up in her favorite chair with her Bible.

I love thee, O Lord, my strength.
The Lord is my rock and my fortress and my deliverer,
My God, my rock, in whom I take refuge;
My shield and the horn of my salvation, my stronghold.
I call upon the Lord, who is worthy to be praised,
And I am saved from my enemies.

The words sunk deep and spread like a balm through her, loosening the cords of frustration and giving her strength. David had been a soldier. She felt a common bond with him. He had been called at a young age to stand against evil. He knew what is was like to be pursued. To be afraid.

You were his refuge. His shield. And You are mine, too.

Finn wrote a few paragraphs in her journal and then began lifting her family and friends up in prayer. Looking out the window, she could see the light still glowing in John's room and she prayed for him, too.

The next morning, John was waiting for her by the garage. She tried not to notice that he looked incredible in casual gray chinos and a green-and-gray checked cotton shirt. In his hand was an official-looking leather briefcase.

"Good morning."

"Finn."

"Did you know that Chief Larson made it mandatory for everyone to attend your training session this morning?" Finn asked. "Just so you understand why the guys who'd normally be off duty today are glaring at you."

John slipped into the passenger side of her Jeep. "Thanks for the heads-up."

"Do I get a preview of today's lesson, Agent Gabriel?" She flipped the visor down out of habit and checked her hair, pulled out a tube of her favorite lipstick and then saw the look on John's face. "What?"

"You're primping," he said in disbelief.

"But never while I'm driving." She flashed him a saucy grin.

That remark was rewarded with one of John's reluctant smiles.

"I'm going to give a mini-seminar on Internet crime," he said. "Computers are like anything else— they can be a weapon in the wrong hands. Law enforcement has to keep up with the changing technology or the criminals have an advantage."

Finn glanced at him. "Is this your area?"

"One of them," John admitted.

"Your favorite?"

He shrugged, but she had seen the spark flare in his eyes. The spark of passion for an area of his chosen career.

"What's yours?" he asked. "Besides trying to get little old ladies safely across the busy streets of Miranda Station?"

How to answer that unexpected question... Finn turned the car into the parking lot of the police station. "I guess I haven't been an officer long enough to find out."

She wasn't about to tell John that there were too many days that her job was frustrating. She was only a small cog in the wheel of law enforcement. If she made an arrest, it went to the DA, who determined whether there was enough evidence to prosecute. If she made a referral to Social Services, then a case worker took over and made a determination. Too many times she felt as if she were wearing her own handcuffs. It was one of the unexpected struggles she'd faced since becoming a police officer. One she hadn't voiced to anyone but God.

They got out of the car and walked toward the station. John suddenly paused just outside the doors.

"I've got to make a phone call. You can go in without me."

"All right." Finn wondered about the quicksilver change in his mood. She had the feeling that John didn't make it a habit to share much of himself, but for a brief moment during their conversation in the car, it felt as if they'd had a connection.

Then again, maybe she'd only imagined it.

John waited until she had disappeared inside, pulled out his cell phone and called time-and-temperature, then walked in alone. He didn't want any of the guys Finn worked with to see them come in together. He couldn't let anyone think he and Finn were friends if he was going to try to get a handle on what was going on with her at the P.D.

The small conference room had been set up for his presentation, and Finn was right—the looks he got when he walked in told him exactly what some of them thought about being called in on their day off.

Finn was already sitting in the front of the room, an empty chair on either side of her. The rest of them were filled. After that one brief glance, John didn't look at her again.

He spent two hours updating them on the latest ways to use computers to catch criminals and another hour answering their questions. After the first fifteen minutes of his talk, there was a change in the room. Even the most disgruntled officer was leaning forward, listening intently. John judged his presentation a success by that one officer. Carl Davis. Davis also asked the most questions. When Finn asked a question, however, he noticed two of the officers behind her look at each other. One of them rolled his eyes and the other, Wes

Garrett, smirked. It was an intelligent question, show-ing that Finn had been paying attention, but he couldn't show his approval.

Still, the temptation to make the guys eat their ASP batons was great.

The officers drifted away when the session was over, and Finn approached him while he was packing up his materials.

"Thank you. Your presentation was great."

He shrugged off her praise. "Part of the job. And now I owe Seamus one less favor."

"He never worked here, but you'd think he'd run the department at one time," Finn said. "He and Chief Larson are golfing buddies."

Another interesting tidbit of information that might explain why Finn was hired, John thought. He slowed his movements, waiting for the room to clear.

"Go ahead and take my car home," Finn said. "I'll get dropped off at the end of my shift anyway." She handed him her keys.

"Thanks."

Mike Alloway appeared in the doorway. "Kelly, I need you to mail some evidence to the crime lab. Think you can find your way to the post office?"

"No problem." Finn smiled sweetly.

"Great presentation, Agent Gabriel," Mike said. "Chief Larson was hoping we could set up another one with you."

"I should be able to do that." John read the officer's name on the silver tag under his badge and remembered it. It had sounded like he'd been teasing Finn with his question about the post office, but it was hard to tell.

So, some of the guys obviously didn't accept Finn as an equal. That was clear enough. But was she so thin-skinned that it would take such an obvious toll on her? One that had caused Seamus to get him involved?

Chapter Five

~∾

The telephone rang, waking Finn up from a sound sleep. She fumbled for it in the dark, her gaze already focusing on her grandparents' house. The last time she had gotten a phone call in the middle of the night, Seamus had had another heart attack.

"Hello?"

"Finn, it's Donna at the P.D. There's another fire and they need some extra people on."

Finn closed her eyes in relief at the sound of the dispatcher's voice.

"Sure." She glanced at the clock beside the bed and almost groaned. Two in the morning. "I'll drive myself in."

"Go right to Fifth and Walnut," Donna directed briskly.

Finn pulled out a clean uniform shirt and pants and dressed quickly. Fifth and Walnut. She sent up a prayer of thanks that it wasn't a residential area. She walked quickly toward the garage, rounded the corner and bumped into something solid.

"Finn?"

"John." She stepped back. "What are you doing out here?"

He didn't answer. "Where are you going?"

"They called me back in to work because there's a fire."

"How much sleep have you had?"

"Three hours," Finn said, already moving toward her vehicle.

"I'll tag along."

"That's not necessary." She paused when she glanced up and saw his expression. "All right. Suit yourself."

The address the dispatcher had given Finn was just past the downtown business district, and as they got closer, the crimson glow from the burning building was visible from two blocks away. Black smoke billowed into the sky, shielding the stars from view.

Finn searched for a familiar face and finally saw Wes Garrett moving along the perimeter. He didn't look very happy to see her.

"Kelly, we've got a bunch of people who'd rather watch this building burn than sleep. Can you believe it? Tape the driveway and then stand here to make sure no one gets past. There's a reporter from the newspaper already trying to squeeze in."

"What happened?" Finn had to lift her voice above the noise of the fire hoses pumping water. Already her eyes were watering and she could taste the smoke.

"We're not sure, but the fire inspector has been called and he'll be here shortly. There's a bunch of stuff stored in this warehouse—maybe something flammable. Who knows?" Suddenly, Wes noticed John Gabriel standing several feet behind Finn. "Hi, John. Felt like losing a little sleep, too, huh? Kelly, make yourself at home—you'll be here a while.'' He disappeared into the hazy darkness.

For a moment, Finn just stared at the blaze. There was a panicked cry from the bystanders when one of the walls caved in, but the firefighters were clear. Most of the people watching were still in their pajamas. Finn scanned the faces of the onlookers until her gaze rested briefly on one of them. It was a young male, tall and thin, his shoulders slightly slumped. Even from the distance that separated them, Finn thought she recognized Ricky Calhoun. She took a few steps toward him, but the wind shifted and smoke poured between them. When she got close enough to recognize individual faces, the person she had thought was Ricky had disappeared.

''Is something wrong?'' John was at her shoulder, so close that his breath stirred her hair.

''No, I just thought I saw someone I know.'' She peered into the darkness, hoping for another glimpse of him. ''I guess not. I better get this tape up.'' She remembered the careless way Ricky had flipped the cigarette into the street when their paths had crossed. She knew the Calhouns lived several miles outside of Miranda Station in one of the most expensive subdivisions. Their home was brand-new and the showcase of a successful businessman. Given the warehouse's location, it was interesting that Ricky would be one of the bystanders at the fire.

Two hours later, the blaze was out and daylight was soaking into the horizon. Finn was exhausted. The building was a total loss.

''Gone,'' she murmured. ''The devastation is incredible, isn't it?''

"Yes, it is," John agreed tightly.

She heard the change in his tone and looked at him, then guessed what he was thinking.

"I'm sorry. I didn't realize…"

"How can you not realize?" he asked, his eyes narrowed. "Don't you see the scar? Everyone else does."

Finn swallowed hard. His eyes glittered like emeralds and his voice was low, but his words cut into her like the flick of a whip. "I see the scars here." She reached up and touched the front of his shirt. "These are the only ones I see."

He caught her hand and she felt the warmth of his skin. For a moment they stared at each other. Finn's heart began to pound in an uneven rhythm.

"I'm going to go back now," he said, breaking the silence. "Don't worry about Colin, I'll let him out."

"Go ahead and take my Jeep," Finn said. "I've got to go back to the station anyway and write out a report, so I'll catch a ride home with one of the guys."

He hesitated for just a moment, then turned and strode away.

John had found Seamus and Anne already awake and sitting at a table on their patio when he arrived. Both had been anxious to hear about Finn. He had accepted a cup of coffee and a slice of Danish, and had told them about the warehouse.

"Arson," Seamus said. "We've had a string of fires lately but no one can figure out who it is."

"They'll get him," John said. "This is a small city. He'll make a mistake."

"Hopefully not on someone's house." Seamus closed his eyes, obviously reliving the past—the sound of the explosion and the strangling smoke.

John knew what he was thinking. He didn't break into a cold sweat anymore when he heard the sound of sirens but it was something he had buried deep within himself.

"I'm going to shower and take Colin out," he said, rising from the wicker chair.

"Finn will be exhausted," Anne fretted. "It's a good thing she's got the next three days off so she can rest up."

Three days off. It would be the perfect time to do some more digging. If she was still talking to him.

This was becoming impossible. He still felt the touch of her hand on his chest. *These are the only ones I see.* Without thinking, he touched the side of his face and remembered Kristen's expression the first time she'd seen him after the bandages had been removed. He'd seen the flare of sorrow in her eyes before she'd looked away. Funny, but he'd immediately sensed that the sorrow was for herself more than for him. Because if she married him, she'd be sentenced to a lifetime of staring at his burned skin.

And what did Finn know about scars? A twenty-three-year-old who had grown up in the shelter of a large, loving family?

Finn went back to the department after her relief showed up. Gil was at the desk. She skirted past him while he was studying the computer screen and went into the back office.

The Juvenile files were closed to the public, but she scanned them briefly and found what she was looking for. Ricky Calhoun. It wasn't a long report, but it was enough.

Carl poked his head in the doorway. "Need a ride home, Finn?"

"Sure. Just a minute." Finn closed the file.

"Looking for something in particular?" he asked curiously as they walked out to the parking lot.

"Not really." Finn hesitated and glanced at him as she slid in the passenger side of the squad car. "I was checking to see if we have anything on Ricky Calhoun."

"Ricky Calhoun?" Carl repeated the name in surprise. "Why?"

"I think I saw him last night at the scene."

"And?"

"I have a hunch."

"A hunch."

"I think that Ricky Calhoun has been setting the fires."

Carl gave a burst of amazed laughter. "You aren't serious…Finn, you can't be serious!"

"He started a fire in a Dumpster when he was a freshman in high school," she told him.

"And that's the basis for your hunch?" Carl was grinning. "Finn, that was years ago!"

Finn was beginning to wish she had never mentioned it. "He's bored. He hangs around doing nothing." As she voiced her thoughts out loud, she realized how thin her suspicions were.

"Finn, that kid is the son of the man who practically runs this city. Even if you had a picture of Ricky Calhoun standing outside a burning building, holding a match and wearing a T-shirt that said 'I love the smell of smoke,' it wouldn't get past the DA's office." Carl turned the squad car into her driveway and looked at her. "A hunch isn't enough for this one, kiddo."

"Maybe if you and I went to the Chief—"

Carl held up one hand. "Whoa, slow down. I'm not going out on a limb with you on this one. Not without solid proof. Look, I know you feel like you have to prove yourself, but if you're wrong and this back-fires…" His index finger made a slicing motion across his neck.

"I know." Finn grabbed her logbook and shoved it in her bag. "See you next week."

Carl stuck his head out the window. "Did you forget that his dad is on the Police and Fire Commission?"

"No," Finn muttered, raising her hand in a half-hearted wave. "I didn't forget."

The house was quiet when she opened the door. No Colin. She realized that John must have taken him over to the other house and was relieved at having no demands placed on her for the moment.

Maybe it was crazy to think that Ricky Calhoun had anything to do with the fires. He was just a kid, not a professional arsonist. If it was him, the fire inspector would have figured it out by now. No wonder Carl thought the smoke had gotten to her. Still, the feeling was so strong.

You can't always trust your feelings.

She tried to push the thoughts from her mind and took a quick shower to get rid of the smell of smoke that still clung to her skin. Putting on her swimsuit and a matching pair of shorts, she stepped outside. When she slipped in through the patio doors of the big house, she found her grandmother in the kitchen, making chicken salad.

"Hi, sweetheart!" Anne hugged her. "John told us all about the fire. Did you just get home?"

"About half an hour ago. Chief said my eight hours

started when I was called in for the fire, so that gives me the rest of the day off.'' She found a spoon and sampled the salad. ''A total loss, but no one was hurt and the fire didn't spread to other buildings.''

''Have some more,'' Anne offered. ''I'll bet you haven't eaten since last night.''

''Just coffee and a stale doughnut,'' Finn admitted.

''John took Colin for a walk a little while ago. They should be back any minute. It looks like you're going to take a swim. It's a beautiful day for it.'' Anne chatted as she cleaned up the kitchen. ''I have to get my hair done and then Seamus is taking me out for dinner tonight. He invited John along, but he said he'd prefer to stay here. The man keeps to himself, doesn't he. I remember after the accident we invited him to family get-togethers and such, but he wouldn't come.''

''Doesn't he have any family?'' Finn asked.

Anne shook her head. ''He was moved around to different foster families most of his life, that's all we know.''

Finn's heart ached for him. She couldn't imagine growing up and being shifted around from place to place. The Kellys were woven tightly together and no matter how large they got or how much distance separated them, the fabric of family was never weakened.

''Your grandpa took John under his wing after the accident. He was the one who talked to the powers-that-be at the Madison Agency to hire him. John got in and, within a few months, started to make a name for himself all on his own.''

Finn wasn't surprised. Gritty determination was evident in every line on the man's face.

They both heard a sharp bark, and Anne looked out the kitchen window. ''They're back.''

Finn's insides fluttered crazily again. She wondered if he was still angry with her. For some reason, honesty won out when she was with John Gabriel. She couldn't help it that she didn't notice the scar on his face when she looked at him.

He hasn't let You heal the things in his past yet, has he, God? Or let them be used for Your purposes? Do whatever it takes to help him open the door to Your love.

Chapter Six

When John walked into the kitchen, both the women looked guilty. Finn's cheeks flushed two shades lighter than her hair and Anne started scooping up bowls of salad. They had been talking about him.

"Thank you for taking Colin out," Finn said, an odd formality in her tone.

John was frustrated. If he was ever going to find out what was going on—if there *was* something going on—then he couldn't let his personal feelings show. Normally, that wasn't a problem, but something about Finn unsettled him. Now, she looked skittish, and uncomfortable, no doubt remembering the conversation they'd had at the fire scene.

"Have some lunch, John." Anne pushed a bowl of chicken salad toward him. "Seamus is resting and then we're going out for the afternoon."

"It's eleven o'clock, Gran," Finn said suspiciously. "Why is Chief resting? Isn't he feeling well?"

"Oh, he's just a little tired today." Anne smiled, and John thought it looked forced.

"Are you sure?" Concern for her grandfather drained the little bit of color from Finn's face, and there were dark smudges under her eyes from lack of sleep.

"Don't worry, sweetheart." Anne patted her arm comfortingly. "I better wake him up if I'm going to make my hair appointment on time. You two enjoy the pool."

She left the kitchen, and Finn stared after her worriedly.

"Finn?"

"Hmm?"

"Look at me."

She did.

"Get some rest."

Her smooth brow furrowed. "I'm fine."

"Douse yourself with sunscreen, grab one of those chairs by the pool and nap for an hour."

Some spark of life came back into her eyes. "Giving orders, Agent Gabriel? I wasn't aware that I was under your supervision."

He hid a smile. She had a way of getting to him, all right. "Technically, I'm a lieutenant, so I outrank you."

"Yes, sir." She gave him a saucy salute before she turned toward the door.

Finn's afternoon rest was cut short by a bank of clouds that moved in, drawing a dark curtain between her and the sun. A cool breeze swept across her, prickling her skin. She grabbed her beach towel and pulled it around her shoulders just as thunder growled in the distance. A quick glance at her watch revealed she had been dozing for about an hour.

There was no sign of John, who hadn't come outside even after her grandparents left earlier. Colin was sleeping under one of the deck chairs.

"Colin, come."

The dog sprang to his feet and followed her back home.

By the time she changed her clothes, the sky was so dark it looked like it was dusk instead of the middle of the afternoon. She lit a few candles and decided to make lasagna for supper. She enjoyed cooking and never minded making extra to take over to her grandparents.

There was a knock on the door and Finn's heart lifted. There was only one person it could be. The one who'd been in her thoughts all afternoon.

"Anne asked me to give you your mail when you woke up." John stood just outside, a thin stack of envelopes in his hand.

"My mail comes to them. Technically, this house is part of the same address." Finn wondered if she was rambling, but she was glad to see him. She couldn't deny it.

"Do you…" Her voice was suddenly drowned out as the heavens opened and it started to pour.

Laughing, she pulled John into the house. "Bad timing, John, it looks like you're stuck here for a while."

"Oh, I don't know," he said slowly. "Maybe I planned it this way."

Suddenly Finn stopped laughing. Every breath that she took for granted was suddenly struggling to get out.

"Why would you do that?" she asked. "Do you like spending time with me?"

There it was again. Her honesty pushing him into a corner and making him aware of things he thought he had buried. Things like feelings. And needs.

A crooked spike of lightning made the lights flicker and distracted Finn for a moment. John took the opportunity to escape. He wandered into the kitchen and saw the beginnings of an Italian dinner. *Coward,* he told himself.

"Lasagna," she said behind him. "You're welcome to stay."

For how long? He shook the thought away even as it surfaced. "Where's your television?"

She studied him. "You don't watch television, do you?"

"Never."

"Quit trying to get out of kitchen duty." Finn rummaged through a drawer by the stove. Out came a square of sunny yellow cloth. Before he could react, he was wearing an apron emblazoned with the words "For This I Went to College?"

He looked at her. "Cute."

"It was a gift from my cousin last Christmas, but I think it looks better on you." Finn flounced away and started to rip up a head of lettuce.

He sighed. "I'll set the table."

"Great." With that simple word, she accepted his presence in the kitchen.

John watched her for a moment.

"Agent Gabriel, it's not polite to stare."

He set the table.

The storm didn't subside. Outside, the wind lashed at the trees and blew rain like shot against the windows. At seven o'clock the telephone rang.

"Hi, Chief...I was thinking about that, too. No, it's fine. John had supper with me. Yes, he's still here. I'll see you in the morning, then." Finn hung up the phone.

"They ended up at the Silvermans' after dinner to play cards and they decided to wait out the storm there."

"That's probably best," John agreed. "Visibility is nil out there."

Colin went to the door and whined.

"No walk tonight," Finn told him.

He recognized the word *walk* and looked at her hopefully.

"Not tonight, boy."

"You shouldn't run at night." John frowned, his gaze raking Finn's slender frame. She couldn't weigh more than a hundred pounds.

"Miranda Station is perfectly safe." Finn chuckled.

"There is nowhere on this earth that is perfectly safe."

"I'm fine, John." Finn started to walk toward the window when suddenly she was lying on her back, staring into John's green eyes. She was pinned to the floor by his arm as he knelt beside her. His face was inches from her own.

"See, anything can happen."

"That's not fair, you took me by surprise," she complained.

"You should never be taken by surprise," he countered. "Didn't they teach you that in recruit school?"

"They taught me to never turn my back on the *bad* guys."

"You don't always know who the bad guys are, do you."

His words cut into her deeply. No, she didn't know. If she did, reports wouldn't change and court notices wouldn't disappear into thin air.

"And are you one of the bad guys?"

"I might be." He released his hold on her and rose to his feet. He extended his hand, but she ignored it and scooted into a sitting position.

Colin trotted over and pushed his face against John's leg.

"Traitor," Finn muttered. Tucking a loose strand of hair behind her ear, she grudgingly accepted his hand and let him pull her to her feet.

"Never let your guard down," he said tersely.

"That's your code, not mine."

"It's every officer's," John argued. "I knew an officer who was off duty and went into a convenience store for a gallon of milk. The place was being held up and he walked right into the middle of it."

"What happened?" Finn asked, but she was afraid she already knew the answer.

"The guy who was robbing the place recognized him first and fired."

Finn turned away. "I don't need to hear any more."

"I think you do," John said, his voice harsh. "Don't you see how fragile you are? How easy it was to take you down?"

Tears stung Finn's eyes. "I'm not expecting a friend to attack me." Even as she said the words, she realized that that was what was happening at the department.

"Finn, some people just pretend to be your friend."

Chapter Seven

Finn slept late the next morning. It was something she seldom did and she recognized it for what it was—an escape from the reality of the evening before. John had left shortly after he'd confronted her about letting her guard down.

She rolled over and closed her eyes. *Lord, he needs to meet You. He needs to learn to trust again. I know You can help him. I know it. Do what You need to do to chip away at the walls.*

When peace started to quiet the churning inside, she got up, showered and dressed. The rain had ended sometime during the night and already patches of blue sky were showing through the clouds. When she walked outside, everything smelled fresh and water pinged gently from the eaves to the flagstone at her feet.

Seamus was standing on the patio in his bathrobe, holding a cup of coffee. He waved a greeting.

"Hi, Chief."

"Feeling rested this morning?"

"Not really," she said simply, mentally reliving the restless night she had spent. "But I'll sleep better tonight."

"So will I," Seamus admitted. "I think I counted raindrops until two in the morning."

"Three."

They both laughed.

"Your day off today," Seamus mused.

"My day off?" Finn teased. "I'm going to mow the lawn when it dries, do some grocery shopping and laundry and weed the flower beds."

"Do you want a cup of coffee?"

"No, thanks." Finn guessed that John was already up and she wasn't ready to see him yet. "I better start my day." Calling herself a coward, she cut a wide path around her grandparents' house to the garage and made her escape.

John heard the Jeep pull into the driveway and he glanced out the window. Finn had finally returned. He was restless and edgy, and he wanted nothing more than to pack up his suitcase and head back to Chicago. And he had told Seamus that only minutes before.

"I'm not getting anywhere," he'd told Seamus flatly. "She is as likely to confide in me as she is to the guy at the gas station. Just sit her down and ask her if something's going on. Believe me, she is honest." It came out sounding like a curse. "She'll tell you."

Seamus had studied him for a few moments. "You want to leave."

"I *have* to leave," John corrected. "I have an investigation going on that other people are taking care of until I get back."

Seamus suddenly looked tired. "I understand. I was just hoping that the two of you..." His voice trailed off and he smiled slightly. "Crazy, I guess. Got too much time to think about things when you're retired."

John couldn't believe what he was hearing. "You were hoping the two of us would *what?*" Okay, his voice rose slightly but he couldn't help it. Had this whole thing been some lunatic plan to link him and Finn romantically?

"Two people that mean a great deal to me," Seamus said defensively. "Is that so crazy? I still think Finn's been distracted by something at work. Larson is too close a friend to confide in, and I don't want him to think Finn can't cut it as an officer. That certainly isn't true."

John was still trying to make sense of the fact that there had been an ulterior motive in Seamus's scheme. He didn't know if he should be flattered or furious.

"You don't know what it's like to feel like you're going to leave loose threads," Seamus said, his voice sounding almost uncertain. "Don't tell Anne, though, she'd string me up in the apple tree over there."

Reminded of Seamus's failing health, John felt his anger drain away. He knew he had disappointed Seamus, but it was getting too difficult to be around Finn and he didn't want to analyze why.

"I'll stay for a few more days," he said, relenting. "Chief Larson already asked me to do a second presentation and wants to give me a tour of the department. If you really think Finn's got a problem there, I'll have an easier time seeing it if I actually talk to some of the officers she works with."

"Whatever it takes, John. You're the expert."

Expert.

For an expert, he felt totally out of his league. He'd rather meet a two-hundred-pound mugger in a back alley than an idealistic twenty-three-year-old cop. At least he knew how to handle the mugger.

Now, watching from his bedroom window, he could see Finn was halfway to her house when a rust-pocked black car pulled up in front of the house and stopped. John tensed and leaned forward as a man got out and sprinted toward Finn. She was unaware of his presence until he was three or four yards behind her. John felt totally helpless. How could she be so unaware of what was happening behind her? And here he was, looking out a second-story window and knowing it would take at least two minutes to get down to her.

The young man was closing in fast when Finn turned and saw him. He was not much taller than she was, but built like a linebacker. John heard her cry from where he watched and his fingers worked to open the window. At least the guy would know someone was watching.

Unexpectedly, the man picked her up and swung her around exuberantly, like a puppy with a new toy. Finn's delighted laughter reached him as he watched, frozen in place. Gradually, his heart rate decreased and he realized that the man was far from a threat. He acted more like a boyfriend.

John watched as Finn wriggled out of the man's embrace and smiled at him, linking her arm through his as they walked the rest of the way to her house together and disappeared inside.

John looked down at his missing arm. Most of the time, he didn't notice it wasn't there. But there were moments when he felt its absence keenly. Watching Finn being swung up into the strong arms of the stranger had been one of them.

* * *

Finn and the young man emerged from the house an hour later, each holding a glass of iced tea. John had been sitting at a table on the patio, trying to concentrate on some paperwork and trying *not* to think about his conversation with Seamus.

"Hi." Finn glanced away when she saw him, which told John she was still uncomfortable about the night before.

"Finn."

"John, this is Ryan. Ryan, John."

Ryan grinned and extended his hand. Reluctantly, John shook it.

"Nice to meet you, John."

The guy looked like he actually meant it, and John nodded coolly.

"I'm going to tell Gran and Chief you're here. Go sit by the pool and soak up some sun, Ryan." Finn was smiling widely as she went in search of her grandmother.

"Join me?" Ryan asked easily.

The two men fell in step together. Colin came bounding up, and as Ryan drew back, preparing for the assault, the dog sat down and tilted his head.

"Whoa! What happened to you?" Ryan asked with a laugh. "Are you finally learning some manners, you old renegade?"

Colin barked and nudged Ryan's hand.

"Come on." Ryan included the dog in their party as they headed to the chairs by the pool. "When Finn first got Colin, he was a mess. He'd started training as a K-9, but his trainer wasn't a pleasant person. Colin just couldn't get the commands—or wouldn't, I suppose. They were going to put him down, and Finn heard about it. She doesn't exactly have room for a German shepherd in that dollhouse she lives in, but she wanted to adopt him. They wouldn't let her. He was starting to snap and growl at people, and they thought he was a high risk. But Finn didn't give up. She asked for a month to prove that he was worth saving. It didn't even take that long. The dog just needed some attention and gentleness. They ended up letting her keep him.''

"He's undisciplined," John said, his lips quirking as Colin looked at him reproachfully, almost as if he understood their conversation.

Ryan shot him an odd look. "He's coming around. Last time I was here, Colin was a tornado. Finn tends to spoil him. I think she's overcompensating for him being mistreated."

"Yes, he's coming around," John agreed. *With a firm hand and a pocketful of biscuits.*

Ryan gulped his iced tea down with obvious pleasure.

"Are there little flowers in that?" John couldn't help asking.

"Yup." Ryan peered into his glass. "I forget what they're called."

"Violets."

Ryan chuckled. "The voice of experience, hmm? I think I'll go in and find out what's taking so long. I threw Finn's schedule off for the day by showing up. Now I'm going to really disrupt things by telling her I'm taking her out for dinner tonight."

Something twisted inside John. Of course Finn would be attracted to someone as open and friendly as Ryan Whatever-His-Name-Was. And the modest gold cross hanging around the guy's neck was a pretty good indication he shared Finn's faith.

With a friendly "catch you later," Ryan excused himself and disappeared into the house to track down Finn. John decided this would be a good time to drive downtown, talk to Chief Larson and get a tour of the Miranda Station Police Department. He had a job to do. And the sooner he could put Chief's fears to rest, the sooner he could leave.

The department was efficiently run and obviously a source of pride for Larson. He was eager to point out what last year's budget had bought, and John listened politely, waiting for the right moment to bring up Finn.

The moment came when they paused in the corridor and John noticed a department photograph on the wall. Finn's face gazed back solemnly at him. She was surrounded by a group of men in blue uniforms. "How is Finn Kelly adjusting?"

Chief Larson frowned briefly. "Kelly? Just fine. We're a progressive department, you know."

John could picture him repeating those words to the mayor or the city council.

"Other than that incident recently with Lessing, she's been right with the program."

Back up the truck. "Lessing?"

"Just a few days ago she missed a court appearance and the judge let a wife beater go free. She claimed she never got the notice, but the dispatcher remembers putting it in her box." Larson shrugged. "I can't tolerate mistakes like that very often."

John immediately put a timeline to the chief's words and came up with the day they were at the range. Maybe her inability to focus had been the result of being afraid to admit she had misplaced or forgotten the notice.

"Excuse me." Larson saw the secretary waving a

piece of paper at him. "Time to get back to work. Feel free to look around some more. There's coffee in the break room."

John glanced once more at the photograph on the wall and then headed in the direction of the coffee. Before he was noticed, he could see several officers sitting together at a long table. One of them was Wes Garrett. He was the kind of cop John had never been able to tolerate. It was easy to discern that his arrogance and his badge covered a multitude of insecurities and prejudices.

"Good thing there wasn't anything flammable stored in that building," one of them was saying.

"I'm glad I didn't hear the phone ring," another added, yawning.

There was a collective snort of disbelief. "What happened, did you forget to take your earplugs out?"

"So who'd they call in?"

"Alloway, Scott, the Meter Maid and Paracheck," Wes said.

The Meter Maid? John stiffened. He had to be referring to Finn. After a moment, when no one called Wes on the derogatory name, John sauntered into the room. The conversation skidded to a halt.

"Good morning." He helped himself to a cup of coffee.

"Morning, Agent Gabriel." Wes recognized him immediately and the others murmured a polite greeting. "We didn't miss another training session, did we?" The others laughed with him.

"Call me John. Your chief just gave me the grand tour. Looks like a nice, tight department."

Wes straightened even more, as though taking credit for John's observation. "Probably different from what you're used to, though. You guys travel a lot, don't you?''

''Enough.'' John pulled out a chair and sat down. He saw Wes glance at his missing arm and then look quickly away.

''Who ate all the cookies?'' one of them complained, delving into the box in the center of the table.

''You snooze, you lose.'' Wes grinned. ''I'll have Carrie bake some more tomorrow.''

''Great, I'm off duty tomorrow.'' The cop shot a look at John in a belated attempt to include him. ''Wes's wife bakes the best cookies. She should open her own bakery.''

''No way.'' Wes shook his head. ''She's my private baker.''

''Barefoot and in the kitchen, huh?'' another chortled.

John felt sickened by the conversation. He listened to their banter for a few more minutes and then excused himself from the group.

No one had batted an eye when Wes referred to Finn as the ''Meter Maid.'' It had to be a nickname they were accustomed to hearing or there would have been some kind of response. He had known cops like Wes since he'd started in law enforcement, but that didn't mean the guy was trying to sabotage Finn's job. He would be risking his own career in the process, and people like him were too smart for that. No, Garrett would vent his hostility toward Finn in the break room, where the most trouble he would get into would be a verbal reprimand if one of the supervisors overheard him.

Larson's words played back through his mind. So, Finn had forgotten a court appearance. Somehow that was tough to swallow. She seemed organized and efficient. He had seen her cupboards. The canned goods were practically in alphabetical order. She didn't strike him as the type to forget something so important.

The thought nagged at him as he drove Chief's car back to the house. The black car was now parked in the driveway, reminding him of their unexpected company. Ryan was mowing the grass and waved at him cheerfully. Cutting the engine, he wiped off his forehead with the back of his hand.

"She put me to work! Can you believe it?" he complained. "She said if we were going out for dinner tonight, then I had to help her get things done this afternoon."

"Seems a fair trade," John said mildly, seeing that he was joking.

"You're welcome to join us, you know. There's a great pizza place outside of town."

John was surprised at the invitation but didn't show it. "No thanks, I've got some phone calls to make."

If that sounded like a thin excuse, Ryan didn't push the issue.

Finn was in the kitchen unpacking a bag of groceries when he walked into the house. She was wearing a pale yellow dress with a floral pattern but her feet were bare. A pair of brown leather sandals had been casually discarded under the table.

"Oh, hello, John." To his amazement, she actually blushed. "I didn't hear you come in."

He realized he had flustered her and wasn't sure why. "Part of my training."

Finn felt like her arms and legs were suddenly detached from the rest of her body as she awkwardly continued putting her grandmother's groceries away. John didn't look like he was going to leave, either. He actually leaned against the counter and watched her.

She wasn't one to let things stay tense in a relationship for too long. With a sigh, she turned and faced him. "You took me by surprise last night. I'm sorry that our dinner ended on a bad note."

His eyes narrowed. "Don't be."

"But I am," she insisted. "I know that you were just making a point that I needed to be careful." She smiled wryly at him and rubbed the back of her head. "Next time, though, just show me a training video."

John frowned slightly and crossed the distance separating them in two strides. "I didn't mean to hurt you," he said quietly.

His gaze was almost hypnotic as he studied her. Finn caught her breath when his hand lifted and he wove his fingers through her hair and tucked it behind her ear. Then his gaze shifted and he was looking at her mouth. She felt the gentle scrape of his knuckles against her cheek and then he tilted her chin slightly.

"Finn!"

Neither of them had noticed the sudden silence that signaled the mowing was done until they heard Ryan's voice in the foyer.

John's hand fell to his side and Finn turned away from him, as Ryan came into the room.

"Are you almost finished in here?"

"Almost." Finn grabbed a bag of apples and dumped them into a wicker basket on the table. Her hands were trembling.

"Are you sure you don't want to come with us, John?" Ryan grabbed one of the apples and rubbed it against the front of his shirt.

''No, I better make those phone calls I mentioned. Thanks, anyway.'' John glanced at Finn, and she turned her face away from him, but not quickly enough to hide the bloom of color in her cheeks.

This was getting too complicated. Ordinarily, he thrived on complicated, but not in the area of relationships. He wished for the hundredth time that morning that Seamus hadn't hinted about him and Finn becoming a couple.

The few dates he'd had in the last ten years had been the result of Diane Avery's matchmaking attempts and had failed miserably. Somehow, he couldn't get past the memory of Kristen's expression when she'd visited him in the hospital after the accident. Oh, she'd tried to mask her fear and disgust, but he'd seen it. And when he'd told her that he thought it best if they broke their engagement, she hadn't been able to hide her relief, either.

Maybe it had been unfair of him to test her like that. Maybe he should have taken her murmured words of love and continued commitment to heart—but he could see they were coated in guilt and a sense of duty, so his pride wouldn't let him. He'd offered her a way out and she'd taken it. And she walked out of his life without a backward glance, taking his foolish dreams of family with her. He told himself that he should have known better. His life had been splintered at a young age, and Kristen had ground the fragments under her heel when she'd walked out. Right along with the hope he'd first tasted when she'd shyly accepted his proposal.

And now Finn was stirring up those feelings again. When he'd looked into those wide gray eyes the night before, he'd actually grieved for the things he'd lost over the years. He had thought he'd pushed them out of his heart and good riddance—nuisance emotions like hope and trust just got a person into trouble—but he'd actually found himself wondering if time spent with Finn would bring some of them back.

Now he told himself he didn't want them back. Not anymore.

Chapter Eight

The next morning when John came downstairs, he discovered Ryan sitting in a chair on the patio in his bathrobe, a dead giveaway that he'd spent the night at Seamus and Anne's. A book was casually balanced on his knee.

"Good morning, John."

Ryan's cheerfulness obviously flowed through both day and night. John, on the other hand, was cranky until his third cup of coffee.

"Join me?"

John didn't want to but he didn't want to be rude either. "Thanks."

"So, have you figured out what's going on with my sister yet?"

John stared at him. "Sister?"

Ryan leaned forward slightly and the book closed. "My sister. Finn."

"Finn is your sister?" John asked in disbelief.

"Yeah, I figured you knew that." Ryan saw the look on John's face and smiled. "I know, we don't look anything alike, do we. I'm some sort of throwback, I guess. In more ways than one, don't you know? All the Kelly carrot-tops and I took after the Donovan side of the family. One crops up once in a while. If you've ever seen my niece, Dana, she's the most recent black Irish. Fortunately, she doesn't have my lantern jaw.'' Ryan rubbed the offending part and grinned.

''You and Finn are close.'' John was accustomed to getting bits of information, processing them quickly and using them to his advantage. He stated the obvious to continue the conversation.

Now he might make some progress. Siblings. Ruthlessly he squashed the traitorous relief that rippled through him.

''Even though there's five years between us,'' Ryan said. ''I was a preemie. Came out purple with the cord wrapped around my neck and almost took my mother's life at the same time. It didn't take long for me to realize that I was supposed to be the next Kelly to pick up the badge, but I was sick a lot. I think they had Finn for insurance purposes.'' He shook his head. ''She was a surprise. Dad had ordered a boy. He'd already picked out the name Finn, but Mom insisted on Fiona. No one calls her that, though. She was Finn right from the start.''

John found that bit of news interesting. That's why he'd assumed that Chief's family emergency was a grandson—not a granddaughter. ''So she went into law enforcement and you…''

''Oh, I would probably be wearing blue, except the Lord had other plans for me. I messed up my knee in an accident when I was eighteen. A week away from my high school graduation and it was bad enough that I could never pass an agility test. Dad was devastated, but Finn stepped up and told him that she planned on being an officer. Carrying on the family legacy and all that stuff. She was just a kid but she never wavered.''

''Is that what she really wanted?''

''No one even questioned it. She always said so.''

And everyone, including her brother, believed her.

''What do you think?'' Ryan asked, his dark-blue eyes suddenly shaded with concern.

''I think the jury is still out.'' John met his gaze. ''Why did you ask me what was the matter with her?'' He wondered if Seamus had confided in Ryan, too.

''She's not herself. It's hard to put my finger on.'' Ryan shrugged. ''I asked her how she liked her job and she told me about the department. I realized later that she never answered my questions. Finn won't lie. She's not wired that way.''

''So you assume because she didn't answer you that that means something is wrong?''

''Right.'' Ryan moved the book onto the table beside him, and John saw that he had been reading the Bible.

''What do you do now?'' he asked curiously.

''I just finished my last year of seminary in January,'' Ryan said, ''and right now I work at a family shelter in Chicago called The Wild Olive.''

''I work in Chicago, too.'' He was surprised when the words came out of his mouth. He generally didn't give too much personal information.

''Finn told me. The Madison Agency.'' Ryan gave a low whistle underscoring that he was impressed. ''And what are you doing here? Somehow you don't seem like the kind of guy who takes vacations.''

''Your grandparents invited me.'' John couldn't help

but smile at his candid—but accurate—assessment. "I know Chief hasn't been well."

"And you're staying how long?"

"Until next week."

A hint of a smile drew up the corners of Ryan's lips.

"Is there a joke in this somewhere?" John asked mildly.

"Your name," Ryan said absently. When John's eyebrows dipped together, he hurried to explain. "Gabriel—that's one of the angels actually named in scripture. He was the one who appeared to Mary to tell her that Jesus was going to be born."

"Is there some sort of resemblance?"

"Not that I know of, but I've never had the privilege of meeting him." Ryan grinned.

John felt himself warming to the young man. He was as refreshing as his sister. Deliberately, he tried to shut the feelings off. "How long are you staying?"

"Until tomorrow, but I'll be back for the Fourth of July. In fact, the whole Kelly clan is going to be here. Too bad you can't stay longer and meet everybody."

John had been invited to attend Kelly family gatherings for years and had always come up with a convenient excuse. He figured that Seamus wanted to absorb him into the family as a goodwill gesture because of the accident, but he was acquainted with the shadows in his soul enough to know that being surrounded by a loving family would only magnify the empty spaces in his life, not fill them.

"Too bad," John lied.

"Right." Ryan smiled wryly. "You'll have to look me up when you're back in Chicago. Maybe we can get together for lunch."

John felt an unexpected twinge of panic. He had kept

up a relationship with Seamus over the years because the old man refused to give up on him. He didn't want to start another friendship. "Sure."

Ryan shook his head. "You lie pretty convincingly, John."

There was no malice in the words, and John didn't take offense. "In my line of work there isn't a lot of time for socializing." That was the truth.

"Sounds pretty lonely."

"Yes, it does," Finn said, suddenly appearing in the doorway, dressed in gray sweats and running shoes. Her hair was caught up in a loose ponytail.

"Hey, kiddo." Ryan sat up straighter and winked at John. "Eavesdropping again, huh? I thought I broke you of that habit years ago."

"You tried." Finn flopped down in one of the patio chairs and helped herself to Ryan's coffee. She looked at John. "Ryan and a friend of his actually staged a conversation that I was getting a horse for Christmas when I was nine. I was so excited...until Christmas morning when there was no horse underneath the tree."

"She holds a grudge," Ryan said in a stage whisper.

John followed their playful banter with bemusement. Suddenly, a memory stabbed him. Quickly and painfully. He was nine and in his third foster home with his younger sister, Celia. She was only a toddler but she was old enough to know that no matter how much she was shuffled around, her brother was the one permanent fixture in her life. Until the December when they were separated. The social worker had stopped by and told him they were going out for lunch but Celia had to stay behind to take her nap. When she brought him back later that afternoon, Celia was gone. He'd never seen her again. When he was eighteen, he had tried to find her, but the paper trail ended when she was placed with a family in a closed adoption. In the years that followed, he'd tried to convince himself that she had been taken in by parents who loved her enough to consider her their own. His dream of being old enough to take care of her himself had been shattered, but he had convinced himself it was for the best and gone on with his life.

"John, I think you need another cup of coffee."

Finn's voice pulled him slowly back to reality.

Ryan was grumbling. "Has she made you be her running partner yet?"

"No."

"Lucky you."

"Oh, quit complaining and get dressed. You're missing out on the best part of the day."

Ryan disappeared into the house, and suddenly she and John were alone together. Finn played with the empty coffee mug on the table. She hadn't meant to intrude on their conversation and hadn't heard anything before Ryan's suggestion that he and John have lunch when they were in Chicago. She wasn't surprised by John's response. For some reason, she couldn't picture him as a man surrounded by friends.

"Ryan tells me that you're having a big family get-together."

Finn's gaze swung up to his face. "We do that every Fourth of July. The place turns into a zoo but we have fun. I worked two weekends in a row for Keith Parachek so I can have that weekend off. I'm anxious to see all my cousins. You'll still be here, won't you?"

"I don't think so. My plans are to leave early next week."

"I didn't know you had a specific plan."

John almost smiled at the irony of her remark. *She* had been his plan from the start. "I've got to get back to work. I did tour your department yesterday, by the way."

Finn leaned forward in surprise. "You did? I would have taken you through if you'd asked."

"I didn't want to take you away from your brother."

"What did you think?"

"Your chief seems like he's on target. The officers were all having coffee in the back room when I was there." He wondered what Finn would say if she knew the nickname they'd given her.

Finn wasn't surprised. It was a gathering place at shift change and the one area the officers headed to when they wanted to unwind. She didn't spend much time there. She had known from the start that her presence made them uncomfortable. It wasn't anything anyone said to her. The conversations and laughter would die down when she came into the room. Some of them would try to include her, but others would suddenly have something they had to get done and she would find herself alone at the table.

"…he told me about your court notice."

"What?" Finn's attention snapped back to John. "What do you mean?"

"He told me you forgot a court appearance—didn't show—whatever."

"I didn't forget."

"What happened, Finn?"

Finn pressed her lips together. "I don't know."

"You have an idea, though."

"Dispatch said it was put in my box. I never saw

it.'' There. Was he going to accuse her of sloppy police work, too? Tell her she wasn't "focused" enough?

"So what happened to it?"

Finn wondered why he looked so intense. His gaze caught hers, searching for the answer before she gave it. "Something. I don't know. It disappeared."

"Maybe you stuck it in your purse or wrote your grocery list on the back of it."

Finn felt as if he'd struck her. "Leave me alone."

"Court notices don't just disappear."

"Someone took it!" The words were wrenched from her, and after she realized what she had told him, she whirled away and headed toward the safety of the house.

"Oh, no." He caught up with her in two strides and took her arm, turning her around to face him. "That's a pretty strong statement, Officer Kelly. Can you prove it?"

"Let go of me! I can't prove anything!" Finn pulled away from him. "What difference does it make to you?"

"Because Seamus coerced me to come here and find out what's wrong with his little rookie, that's why," John said with quiet force. "And I'm trying to figure out if there really is something going on at the department or if you decided that you had to go into police work to get the heat off your brother, and now you're looking for a way out."

"I don't believe you."

Chief had *asked* John to come to Miranda Station? Because of her? They'd lied to her. *John* had lied to her. All along, the interest he'd shown in the department—in *her*—was a favor to her grandfather. She'd thought that they were becoming friends, but he'd been spending time with her because Seamus had asked him to.

"You could have told me why you were here." The sense of betrayal left a bitter taste in her mouth. "You didn't have to pretend..." She suddenly remembered the day before in the kitchen, when his fingers had skimmed through her hair and touched her face. She'd seen the flare of emotion in his eyes, felt the gentleness in his touch. *I didn't mean to hurt you,* he'd said. Apparently that had been a lie, too. And she didn't doubt for a second that John would use any resource available to him when it came to investigating something.

"Not everyone is cut out for police work, Finn," John said, staring down at her. "Even if your last name is Kelly."

A terrible numbness began to sweep through her. At least this part she could try to make him understand.

"I can't explain what's happening at the department, that's why I haven't told Chief. With his heart problems, I didn't want to worry him. Besides that, everyone treats me well. Oh, I'm not one of the guys," Finn admitted. "I can't prove a thing, though. Numbers don't match on my reports. It looks like I'm not paying attention or that I'm sloppy. I'm starting to think that it's all in my imagination. Maybe I did get the notice...." That was what bothered her the most. Now she was second-guessing herself.

"No, you didn't." John's soft voice pulled her gaze up to his face again.

"I wish you'd tell me whose side you're on," she said in frustration. She saw an expression on his face that she was still too angry to identify. "You're the one who just suggested I'm trying to wreck my own career."

"Finn, if someone was against you being hired, they're not going to put their own neck in a noose by trashing your locker and shredding your reports. Those things are too easy to trace. No, if they can make you look unprofessional, you won't make your probation and no one is the wiser. It'll just look like there was a woman who wasn't cut out for law enforcement. It may even mean they're more cautious about hiring a woman next time."

Finn did see. It was what she had sensed was going on from the beginning.

"You don't know who the bad guys are." She repeated his words with a trace of regret.

"That's right." John wondered why this tiny loss of innocence in Finn was so disturbing. If she really wanted to be a cop, in ten years nothing would surprise her. He had worked on a case early in his career where parents had actually sold their child to a wealthy couple in another country. When he had escorted the little girl back to the United States, she was asking him when she could see her mother. Her *real* mother. He had delivered her into the hands of the authorities and had never asked what became of her. He hadn't wanted to know.

"So what are you supposed to do? Come to my rescue? Just for the record, I already have someone protecting me."

"Who? That overgrown puppy you call a dog?"

"I'm talking about God."

"Sure, God," John said, his eyes narrowing. "So you believe that God answers prayer?"

"Yes, I do." Finn's chin lifted slightly.

"Well, maybe I'm the answer to yours."

Chapter Nine

The telephone rang inside the house, effectively severing their conversation.

"Excuse me." Finn turned away and went to answer it. "Hello?"

"Hello." It was a woman's rather breathless voice. "Is John Gabriel there, please?"

Finn walked back to the window, but there was no sign of him. "Well, he was a minute ago. Can you hang on?"

There was a faint chuckle. "I'm not sure, I'm on my way to the hospital and he promised he'd be here when the baby was born."

Finn felt as if all of the blood in her body turned to ice water. "Who…?"

"I'm sorry! This is Diane Avery." There was a slight gasp on the last syllable of the name, and Finn's hand tightened on the phone. "Can you tell him?"

"I'll tell him." Finn leaned against the counter for support. "Diane Avery."

"Right."

Finn heard a man's muffled voice in the background.

"I'd better go. They say the first one takes forever, but you never know." The woman's voice was strained. "Thank you."

Finn hung up the phone, her feet rooted to the floor. Someone was having a baby. Some strange woman in labor actually called to make sure John Gabriel would be there. He had *promised* her he'd be there.

Ryan appeared in the doorway, his expression concerned when he saw the look on Finn's face.

"Where is John?"

"By the pool." Ryan put out his hand as if to steady her. "Are you all right?"

"I've got a message for him."

John's expression was shuttered when he saw her walking toward him.

"You just had a phone call from someone named Diane Avery. She said she's on her way to the hospital."

The color suddenly drained from his face. "The baby isn't due for two more weeks."

"She said you promised you'd be there."

"I did." John pushed his fingers through his hair and then looked at her intently. "Will you go with me?"

Finn stared at him. "Go with you?"

"I don't have a car here," he reminded her. "They live in Chicago." He glanced at his watch. "We can be there in less than three hours."

Finn only hesitated a moment. "Sure. Let me tell Ryan."

"Pack an overnight bag. I'm not sure how long babies take. Do you?"

Confused as she was about this unexpected situation and still reeling over learning the real reason John had shown up at Chief's, Finn still couldn't help but smile. "Sometimes it's days and sometimes it's in the back of taxis."

"Great," he muttered.

Finn told her grandparents she was going to Chicago with John, tossed some things into a small suitcase, and twenty minutes later they were on their way to Chicago. John stared at the road ahead of them. He had seemed out of sorts since the phone call.

"Who is Diane Avery?"

"What?" He glanced sharply at her and then relaxed. "She's a friend."

A friend. That told her absolutely nothing of importance. Was she the check-out person at the grocery store? His mail carrier? A colleague? Someone special?

"Finn, I'm sorry about blasting you back at the house," he shocked her by saying. "I wanted to shake you a bit to get to the truth. I usually take my time on investigations but you…"

She was an investigation. The thought didn't sit well. She was going to have a long talk with Seamus when she got back.

"…you have a way of rattling me."

Finn gaped at him. "You're kidding, right?" She glanced over and saw his serious expression. "I actually *rattle* the calm, collected Madison agent, John Gabriel?"

"Crazy, isn't it?" He shifted in the seat and turned his attention to the passing scenery.

"If it were true."

John decided not to argue the point. "If you are a

battleship and you know there's a submarine tracking you somewhere below the surface, what do you do?''

''Keep my eye on the radar.''

''Radar is out.''

''Figures,'' Finn grumbled. ''Head to port?''

''Can't.''

''You can always head to port,'' she complained.

''Not this time.''

She was silent for a few minutes, and he could see her frown of concentration.

''I don't know,'' she said.

''Sure you do.''

''Send down another sub and take it out,'' she whispered.

''You have two choices,'' John said, not acknowledging that she had just answered his question correctly. ''You can stay at the department and probably not make your probation, squawk a little about discrimination and move on, or you can start your own hunt for the person who's doing this to you.''

''You still think I don't want to be a cop, don't you.''

''I'm beginning to think that you want to,'' John admitted. ''I'm just not convinced that you're cut out to be one. You remind me of cotton candy, Finn. Real sweet—but let's just not test it against fire or water, right?''

Finn's fingers tightened on the steering wheel in response to his words. His opinion of her cut deeply but she was determined not to show it. And maybe there was a grain of truth in what he said. She remembered the first time she had come face to face with domestic violence. Jerome Lessing. Defiant and menacing even as his wife cowered on the sofa and their daughter stood watching, pale and terrified. Finn had felt sick to her stomach. She knew domestic violence occurred. Had seen the statistics. But nothing could have prepared her for her reaction when Tina Lessing tugged on her arm.

"Are you taking my daddy away?"

She had grown up surrounded by love. On the rare occasions that called for discipline, her father could be stern and unyielding but she always knew she was loved. Her mother, a kindergarten teacher, was kind and soft-spoken. There had been a network of aunts and uncles and cousins who kept a watchful eye on one another, particularly the children.

And then there was John, a foster child with no roots. No family. No one to look out for him.

"Finn?"

His quiet prompting pulled her back and she looked at him crossly. Obviously he was waiting for some response to his comment.

"Don't try to water it down for me, Agent Gabriel. Just say what you mean."

The slashes along his mouth deepened as he tried not to smile. "I guess I've been accused of being direct."

"Really?"

Now he did smile. "Really."

"I won't deny that what you just said hurt," Finn said simply. "But I can see why you might think I'm fragile."

A bomb going off in front of the car wouldn't have startled him as much. Most women would have pouted or gotten angry. But not Finn. There was a quiet dignity in the stiffness of her shoulders. He almost groaned. Whenever he was with her, he felt his equilibrium was off. She said things he didn't expect her to say. Did things he didn't expect her to do. And she was so honest that he almost regretted his words.

"Finn, did you go into law enforcement because Ryan couldn't?"

"Is this our exit?"

John glanced out the window and nodded. "I'm glad one of us was paying attention. The hospital is about a mile down on the left." It wasn't until some time later that he realized she hadn't answered his question.

They were both silent until the hospital came into view. Finn found a parking spot and looked at him expectantly. "I can wait here."

"I'd prefer that you come with me."

Her eyebrows rose. "Sure."

The hospital was full of activity, and they found the maternity ward quickly. When the elevator doors swept open on the fourth floor, John hesitated.

Finn lifted her nose and pretended to sniff the air, frowning slightly. "I think I smell cotton candy."

"You..." John rounded on her with a growl, saw the look on her face and gave her a gentle shake. The leashed strength in his grip made her gulp, although she could tell he was teasing her.

"John!"

They both turned as a man paused in front of the elevator. He was tall and attractive with light-brown hair and a neatly trimmed mustache. His eyes widened in surprise when he saw Finn caught in John's grasp.

"How is Diane?" John stepped out of the elevator, pulling Finn with him as the doors started to close.

"Well, about ten minutes ago she kicked me out of

the room,'' he said cheerfully. ''But that was after we
had a baby girl.''

''A girl.'' John looked suspicious. ''Already?''

Neil laughed. ''Already. You know Diane. I think
sheer determination had a hand in it. She wasn't going
to spend the next twelve hours in labor and that was
all there was to it.''

Finn listened to their exchange with interest. Then,
Neil turned his attention to her.

''I'm Neil Avery, by the way.'' He grinned at her.

''Finn Kelly.''

''Finn drove me here from Miranda Station,'' John
explained.

''I'm glad you did,'' Neil said, his voice pleasant.
''John promised Diane he'd be here.''

''I'm the first official member of the Avery Fan
Club, so I'm told,'' John said.

''What have you named her?'' Finn asked.

John hadn't even thought to ask.

''Deborah Elaine,'' Neil said. ''Elaine is Diane's
mother's name and Deborah was a very special woman
in the Old Testament who led an army.''

Finn's eyes lit up. ''I know who Deborah is. She's
one of my favorite people in the Bible.''

Neil and John exchanged looks over her head. Neil's
smile was smug, and John shook his head. Maybe it
hadn't been such a good idea to bring Finn along after
all.

''They're in here.'' Neil's voice dropped and he
pushed the door open quietly. ''Hey, beautiful. John is
here. With a friend.''

''Bring them in!''

Finn's first impression of Diane Avery was of her
voice. Warm and full of energy. She hung back a little,

feeling just a bit uncomfortable at charging in uninvited, but it was Neil who took her arm and urged her into the room.

"It figures that you couldn't wait fifteen more minutes," John groused at her, although his eyes were full of laughter.

"I'm sorry." Diane Avery looked anything but. She did, however, look radiant propped up against the white pillows, her black hair fanned out behind her. She was more than pretty. She was stunning. Her features had the chiseled look of a fashion model and her skin was the color of warm cocoa. "I couldn't wait another second to meet my daughter."

The nurse walked in with a tiny bundle swaddled in a pink flannel blanket. "She's all yours now, Mr. Avery."

Finn stepped closer as Neil took the baby and cradled her gently in his arms.

"Deborah, say hello to your uncle John," Neil crooned.

"He just calls me that so the kid gets a bigger present at Christmas," John muttered to Finn.

"I heard that," Diane said. "And you should probably scrape up some of the manners I know you have and introduce me to your friend." She smiled at Finn. "I'm sorry, but babies tend to be show-stealers, don't they?"

Caught in Diane Avery's friendly gaze, Finn responded with a smile of her own. "That's the way it should be. I'm Finn Kelly."

"It's nice to meet you." Diane sighed and closed her eyes. "I think I'm tired."

Neil grinned. "You deserve a rest, sweetheart.

Where are you staying tonight, Finn? You are more than welcome to spend the night at our house.''

''She's staying at my apartment,'' John interjected. ''And I'm staying with you.''

''I am?'' Finn questioned.

''You are.''

''I am.'' Finn shrugged easily.

''We'll be back later this evening.'' John amazed Finn when he bent over and dropped a kiss on Diane's cheek. ''Good work, soldier.''

She chuckled, her eyelids drooping sleepily as she gazed at him. ''Thanks for coming.''

He caught up to Finn in the doorway. ''I'll buy you dinner.''

Neil, still brushing kisses against Deborah's rose-tinted cheeks, heard. So did Diane.

''Does he know he's in love?'' she murmured.

''Not a clue. The poor guy.''

''I'd say it's about time,'' Diane said, then promptly fell asleep.

Chapter Ten

There were about fifteen babies lined up in plastic cribs in the hospital nursery, each with a colorful name tag proclaiming to the world who they belonged to. As John and Finn watched, one of the nurses put another pink flannel bundle to sleep.

"I love babies," Finn murmured.

John narrowed his eyes at her. "What part do you love the most? The messy diapers, the colic or the expense?"

"Spoken like a true cynic." Finn nudged him lightly. "I baby-sat a lot when I was in high school. Your friends seem excited. Is Deborah their first child?"

"Probably the first of many, if Diane has her way," John said. "They'll be good parents. They've been trying for several years to have a baby."

John seemed to shy away from relationships, so Finn was surprised that he was close enough to the Averys to know such an intimate detail of their lives. She remembered Chief commenting more than once about what a loner John Gabriel was.

"I'm happy for them," Finn said. "Babies are such a blessing."

"Not everyone feels that way." John turned sharply away from the nursery window and strode toward the elevator.

Finn wondered if he was thinking about his own parents. Hadn't he been a blessing to his mother? Hadn't she cradled him in her arms and cooed at him? Loved him so much it hurt?

They were alone on the elevator and Finn touched his arm. "What's wrong?"

"I was thinking about my sister."

She tried to hide her surprise. "Your sister?"

He laughed but there was no humor in it. "The one thing my mother was able to do was have children. It's just that she didn't know what to do with them *after* she had them. My sister and I were split up and sent to different foster homes when she was two and I was nine. She was adopted later by another family. I was never successful at finding out what happened to her."

"What was her name?"

"Celia."

They reached the first floor and stepped outside. A warm breeze lifted Finn's hair from her shoulders and blew it against John's arm. Self-consciously, Finn pushed it into place. She didn't know what to say. His set expression told her he wouldn't accept her sympathy. His tone warned her not to dig any deeper.

"I feel like Italian food," she said blithely. "How about you?"

"Chinese."

Finn wrinkled her nose. "Compromise?"

"How do you compromise between Italian and Chinese?"

"Greek."

John rolled his eyes. "Sorry I asked. Greek it is."

"Am I really staying at your apartment tonight?"

"You are. By the time we get you settled in at my apartment and go out for dinner, it'll be too late for you to drive back."

Finn hid a smile. "Yes, sir."

"Am I being direct again?"

"No, right now you're being bossy, but I'm too hungry to care."

Finn shouldn't have been surprised at John's apartment. If she'd been given time to consider it, she probably could have guessed what it would look like. Sterile. Sterile and unlived in. She stood in the foyer, clutching the bag of leftovers from the restaurant in one hand as she looked around. John was several feet ahead of her when he finally paused and turned back.

"You can come in, you know."

Finn followed him and tried not to let him see her dismay. The apartment complex he lived in was beautiful. It was on the outskirts of Chicago, made of mellowed brick with willow trees lining the drive. She had imagined burnished woodwork and antique furniture. What she found inside was burnished woodwork and no furniture. Well, there were a few pieces: a lumpy beige couch and a reading lamp, a chair propped against the wall by the telephone but no kitchen table. There were drapes covering the windows but no pictures on the wall. Finn guessed the drapes had come with the apartment.

"I'm not here much," John said. "My work takes me away quite a bit."

"So does mine."

He eyed her. "Do I detect a note of disapproval, Officer Kelly?"

"I hope your decorator is in jail," she said sweetly, "because this place is a crime. I'll be surprised if there isn't a chalk outline on the floor instead of a bed."

John couldn't believe she was criticizing his apartment. And he thought *he* was too direct!

Finn's hands were planted on her slender hips and she looked like she could cheerfully take a match to the place. He glanced around. Maybe it was a bit…sparse. He just didn't have the time or the inclination to furnish his apartment. Diane had hinted several times over the past few years that she'd go shopping with him if he ever needed her to, but so far he hadn't taken her up on the offer. The apartment wasn't important. He spent most of his day at the office, on a plane or in another state.

He thought about Finn's house with its comfortable furnishings and homespun touches. No wonder she looked upset.

"You can call Chief and tell him you're all right." He headed toward the bedroom with Finn's overnight bag, then realized she was following him.

"There *is* actually a bed in here," she declared. "I thought maybe you slept in your briefcase."

John tried not to laugh. She looked so offended. Why she would take his furnishings, or lack thereof, so personally, he couldn't figure out. "Do you want to go back to the hospital with me or are you too tired?"

"I'll stay here."

Finn sounded distracted, and he put his hand on her shoulder to get her attention. She tipped her head back to look up at him—and suddenly he couldn't breathe. Her eyes, that soft shade of pewter gray, were wide as they met his. There was a question in their depths. He glanced up and caught their reflection in the dresser mirror.

Her hair was curling down her back, escaping the loose braid she had used to confine it earlier. Her skin was smooth, with a translucent glow that defied the need for makeup. And his? Puckered with scar tissue from the fire. But there was more than just the outward appearance. Finn had something *inside,* too. He saw it every time he looked in her eyes. Something that he lacked. He stepped away from her, struggling with his thoughts. There were times when she almost seemed…attracted to him. He glanced in the mirror again and was bitterly reminded that he had nothing to offer someone like Finn.

Her words came back to him. *I don't see the scars on the outside.* That wasn't possible. For ten years he had gotten used to children staring. To people averting their eyes when they saw him. Even his fiancée, who had professed to love him, hadn't been able to see beyond his scars.

"There's a phone on the nightstand," he said, tearing his eyes away from the mirror and summoning the self-control that had kept him alive so far.

Part of his training was to know when it was prudent to escape a dangerous situation.

When the telephone rang at her grandparents' home, it was Ryan who answered.

"Hi."

"Hi, yourself. Did you get John to the hospital on time?"

"Yes and no," Finn said, sitting carefully on the edge of the bed. There was absolutely no movement. She bounced a little and winced. *I'm surprised he doesn't sleep on a bed of nails.* "The Averys had a girl by the time we got there."

"Are you coming back in the morning?"

"I think so." Finn heard movement in the kitchen down the hall and relaxed a little. "Are you going to be there when I get back?"

"Since you're in the Windy City, I thought I'd just drive back and show you around the shelter instead," Ryan suggested. "You haven't seen the place in a while."

"I'd love that." Finn had visited the shelter on other occasions and had realized her brother was the catalyst behind many of the changes. She gave him John's telephone number in case they needed to reach her and then talked briefly to Anne before hanging up the phone.

"Are you sure you don't want to come back to the hospital?" John asked when she found him in the kitchen moments later.

Finn hesitated. She wouldn't have minded getting to know the Averys better but didn't want to intrude. "I think I'll stay here. But please, go ahead."

"Make yourself at...home." John's lips quirked a bit as he emphasized the last word.

"Thank you."

"I'll be back in the morning, but I wrote Neil's address and telephone number down just in case you need anything."

He was brisk and businesslike. And he wouldn't look

at her. Finn wondered why. Maybe she had been too strong in her opinions about his choice of decor.

"Don't apologize," John said, apparently able to read her thoughts. "Not when you're right."

Then he was gone.

Finn wandered over to the window and peered down into the shadowed yard below. The setting sun had brushed a stroke of pale pink against the clouds and already a star winked in the sky. There were voices and laughter from one of the other apartments nearby. Why had he chosen such a pretty complex if he hadn't intended to actually *live* in it?

Still satisfied from dinner, she investigated the kitchen cupboards out of curiosity, clucking her tongue in the silence. It was just as she had suspected. There was a pitiful amount of pantry food and the refrigerator was worse. A bottle of mustard, some cheese and an odd assortment of unlabeled freezer containers. Finn wrinkled her nose. He had said he wasn't much for cooking. Obviously, that was an understatement.

She found a telephone book and made several calls. She would be long gone before he found out what she had done!

She took her Bible out of her overnight bag and curled up on the sofa, tucking her feet underneath her.

Lord, I thank You for Neil and Diane Avery's new baby...she's such a perfect example of Your many blessings! I pray for John...he's had a difficult life. He never knew what a loving family was, and I can see it still affects him now. I know You love him, Lord, but he has so many walls around his heart.

Finn curled up on the lumpy sofa and opened her Bible to the place where she had stuck her pen the night before. She glanced at a passage and then kept reading, her heart beginning to pound. Here were the passages where David was chosen by God to be king of Israel.

"...for God sees not as man sees, for man looks at the outward appearance, but the Lord looks at the heart."

Finn read the verse several times. Samuel was looking over Jesse's sons to see which one had received God's anointing. The future king. No doubt a grown man with some bulk...a street-smart warrior. But one by one the sons of Jesse were rejected, until David appeared. David, who was described as young. And beautiful.

Finn smiled. She knew that when people saw her in uniform, there was a flash of surprise in their eyes. A spark of disbelief. She didn't fit people's expectation of a police officer. She was young, just as David had been when Goliath mocked him on the battlefield. But David's strength had been in God...and that's where she wanted hers to come from.

She sat up just a little straighter. John didn't think she was strong enough, emotionally or physically, to be a police officer. There were times when she doubted it herself, but the words in 1 Samuel reminded her that God looks at the heart.

She had purposely avoided answering John's question about whether she went into law enforcement because of Ryan because she wasn't sure of her answer. She remembered Ryan being sick a lot when he was young, plagued in the winter months with respiratory problems. She remembered hearing Ryan telling their parents about how he had surrendered his life to God after spending a weekend with friends at a youth retreat. And Nolan Kelly had responded by telling him that all the strength he needed was inside himself. Almost dutifully, Ryan had aimed toward a career in law enforcement. Until the car accident that had damaged his knee.

Their father's disappointment in Ryan was so great that Finn, as young as she was, sensed a break in their relationship. It was during that time that Seamus had been injured by a homemade bomb and saved by a young officer in his department. John Gabriel. And Finn had made a decision.

At the hospital, John paced the floor while Deborah Elaine Avery, tucked in the crook of his arm, solemnly studied his face.

"So tell us about Finn Kelly." Diane had had a long nap and was ready for conversation.

"She's Seamus Kelly's granddaughter."

"And?"

"And a police officer in Miranda Station." John wondered why Deborah's brow wrinkled at the sound of his voice. Maybe she was going to cry....

"She's a police officer?" Neil's eyebrows shot up. "I'd have guessed she was still in high school." He winked at Diane behind John's back.

John knew that Finn looked young, but to hear someone else say it made him irritable. "I think she's twenty-three."

"Pretty, though."

"Striking," Diane agreed, adjusting the pillow behind her back.

John looked down at Deborah and shook his head. "Your mother is a hopeless romantic."

Diane grinned. "What did she think of your apartment?"

"She told me my decorator should be in jail."

"I knew I liked Finn Kelly," Diane remarked to Neil.

"She said she was surprised there wasn't a chalk line on the floor instead of a bed and accused me of sleeping in my briefcase."

Neil's shoulders shook and then he gave up and started to laugh out loud. "I'm sorry, but she has a point."

"Hmm." John walked over to Neil and held Deborah out to him, but the other man ignored the gesture. You'd think such a proud father would be anxious to hold his first child, John thought darkly. He gave up and tried Diane. She ignored him, too.

"You keep her for a while. You may need the practice."

"Diane!"

She was the only one who could get away with those outrageous comments. He wasn't sure why he allowed it, except that Diane's personality had the momentum of a freight train. When the Madison Agency hired him, he had tried to avoid a friendship with the Averys, but they never took the hint. Finally, John gave up and, little by little over the years, he had allowed them to pull him into their lives. Dinner once a month. An occasional sporting event with Neil. He had declined their invitations to attend church from the beginning, but they never pushed in that area. They seemed to accept him the way he was, and although he knew he had a reputation at Madison as being aloof and, to some, intimidating, Diane Avery had teased him unmercifully and badgered him from the moment they met. Neil also seemed unaffected by John's moods.

"So when are you coming back to work?" Neil asked.

"Early next week."

"Finished your business already?"

"Just for the record, Finn was my business. Seamus was worried about her and wanted me to use my 'excellent investigative skills' to find out what was wrong. She's being harassed at work by someone and her job is on the line." He didn't mention Seamus's other motive for luring him to Miranda Station. Diane would never let go of that one!

"That's why you went to Miranda Station?" Neil frowned. "Why couldn't he just ask her what was wrong?"

"I wondered that myself...except Finn wouldn't admit there was anything wrong. Seamus's health hasn't been good, and I don't think Finn wanted to add to his concerns." She was constantly protecting the people she cared about. Her brother. Seamus. He wondered if she even realized it.

"So you came clean with her?"

"Yeah." John shrugged and looked down at Deborah, who had fallen asleep. Something twisted inside him. He thought about Celia again. Then he wondered why he had told Finn about her. Not even Neil and Diane knew he had a sister.

"Was she upset?"

John frowned. "Why would she be?"

Diane sighed and slid a weary glance at her husband. "I'm hungry."

Neil rose to his feet and reached out to take his daughter. John handed her over quickly.

"I'll put Deborah to bed and see what they have in the cafeteria," said Neil.

"I'll go with you," John offered.

"Why don't you stay here and keep me company?"

Diane smiled pleasantly, and John felt a stab of dread at the gleam in her eyes.

"Sure."

Finn ordered a pizza. She shouldn't have been hungry after the dinner she'd eaten just hours earlier, but she was. It didn't take long to locate a pizza delivery service in the phone book, and then she curled back up on the couch to wait for it to arrive.

She had found a blanket and an extra pillow in a linen closet and decided to sleep on the sofa, her sweat-suit alternating as pajamas. When the security intercom buzzed, she grabbed some money out of her purse and headed toward the door. John was standing there.

"Oh." She felt her face grow warm. "I thought you were someone else."

His eyebrows rose. "Someone else?"

Just then, a young man bounded up the stairs, filling the entryway with the smell of pepperoni.

"450B?" he asked cheerfully.

"Uh-huh." Finn handed him the money and took the pizza, aware of John watching the exchange with an enigmatic look on his face.

"Pizza?"

She backed into the foyer and he followed her. "I was hungry."

He sniffed the air appreciatively. "Sausage?"

"Pepperoni."

He glanced at his watch. "Ten o'clock. Haven't you heard of indigestion?"

She shrugged. "But we skipped lunch and went straight to supper. So…I am going to count this as lunch. Besides, we Kellys have iron stomachs. I thought you weren't coming back until tomorrow morning.''

''I wouldn't have,'' John said, ''except that Diane started interrogating me at the hospital. Did I tell you where the towels are? Did I make sure you had bedding? All that hospitality stuff.''

Finn grinned. ''I made do.''

''So I see.'' He wandered into the living room and noticed the sofa neatly made up with a navy blanket and sheet. ''You could have slept in the bedroom.''

''Given a choice between lumpy couch or iron mattress, I'll take lumpy couch, thank you very much.'' Finn put the pizza down on the coffee table.

''Are you going to eat that pizza or were you planning to have it for breakfast?''

''Would you like a slice?''

''I never turn down pepperoni.''

His elusive smile surfaced suddenly, and Finn's mouth suddenly dried up. John had the most charming smile. Sort of lopsided with just a shadow of a dimple at the corner of his mouth. Definitely a lethal weapon!

''Ryan is taking me to The Wild Olive for a tour and then out for lunch tomorrow,'' she told him, sitting cross-legged on the floor with the pizza between them.

''I've decided not to go back with you to Miranda Station,'' John said abruptly. ''I called your chief and explained the situation. He said if I come back, to let him know and we can set up another training session.''

''What about your things?'' Finn wondered why she felt a certain emptiness at the thought of driving back to Miranda Station alone.

''We've got a break in a case, according to Neal, that I should follow up on. I'll come back when I get the chance.''

There was silence for a few minutes, each one lost in thought.

"Finn, tell Seamus about the trouble you're having at the department," John advised, his voice brisk. "He may have some ideas. You thought that keeping it from him would save him from worrying, but it made it worse."

"You're right," Finn said quietly. "And thanks for your advice. There is someone at the department I know I can trust."

"Who do you have in mind?"

"Carl Davis. He was my training officer and he's always looked out for me. If I confide in him, he might be able to help me find out who's been trying to get me fired."

"Good enough." John finished off his second slice. "I still can't believe you ordered a pizza."

"And I can't believe you're helping me eat it."

He was totally unashamed. "It's been at least three hours since supper." John rose to his feet and looked down at her. "I'll see you in the morning." He offered her his hand, in much the same way he had the night at her house, and she let him draw her to her feet.

"Thank you for letting me stay here."

He nodded curtly and left her alone. Again. Mocking himself, he wondered if it was wisdom or self-preservation that forced him to put distance between them.

Chapter Eleven

Finn was safely back in Miranda Station by now. John knew that. He had seen her off in the morning and then had returned to the Madison Agency to bury himself in his latest case. For some unknown reason, he had dreaded going back to his apartment that evening. Instead he had stopped at the hospital to visit Diane, had a cup of coffee with Neil in the cafeteria, dutifully jiggled Deborah around the tiny hospital room and then headed home.

There were traces of Finn in his apartment. The sheet and blanket were folded neatly at one end of the sofa. The room still smelled suspiciously like pepperoni. For the first time, the emptiness stung. Almost as if he had gotten used to something and then had it snatched away.

The intercom buzzed. He pressed the button in annoyance, glancing at his watch. "Yes?" he barked into the speaker.

"Uh...John Gabriel?"

"Who is it?"

"Jansen's Floral."

Floral? "You must have the wrong place."

"450B?"

"Come up." John hit the lock on the security door and a few seconds later was greeted by a young woman dressed in a polka-dot shirt. Holding an enormous plant. Or a tree. It looked more like a tree.

"I didn't order this."

"There's a card, mister."

Cautiously, as if it were a bomb, John grabbed the plant. By the time he finished wrestling it into the foyer, the young woman had disappeared.

He set the plant down on the floor and searched for the card.

Put it next to the sofa and don't kill it.

Finn

Muttering to himself, John hauled it into the living room and pushed it into the corner by the sofa.

The intercom buzzed two more times. The second time, it was a delivery person from the grocery story, his arms loaded with several brown bags of food. Healthy stuff. The third time it was a pepperoni pizza. By the time he went to bed two hours later, he was already plotting revenge.

"Colin, get back!" Finn laughed as the dog dodged out of her way. "I'm sorry I left you, but you don't have to shadow me every second."

Colin curled up on the braided rug near the door, eyeing her closely. Ever since she had returned from Chicago, he hadn't been more than six inches away.

She practically tripped over him with every step she took.

"Squad car is here…I know, I know," she said, seeing his ears lift. "Duty calls." She bent down to give him a pat on the head and then slipped out the door.

Carl waved to her as she approached. "How was your time off?"

"Nice." Finn stuffed her gear by her feet, flipped the visor down and checked her hair in the mirror.

"Someone said your brother was visiting."

"He was, but he's back in Chicago now, too."

"Too?"

"I drove John Gabriel back."

"No kidding."

Finn didn't miss the underlying curiosity in his tone but she refused to discuss her relationship with John. It was just as confusing to her.

"Carl, could I tell you something in confidence?"

Without a word, Carl maneuvered the squad car onto the shoulder of the road and stopped. "Go for it."

"Remember that incident with Lessing?" Finn asked. At Carl's nod, she continued. "Well, I never got the court notice, Carl. Someone must have taken it out of my box so it looked like I forgot it. There have been over things, too. Changes made on my reports so it looks like I'm sloppy. Little things, but they could add up so I don't make my probation."

Carl was staring at her. "Those are pretty strong accusations, Finn. That means someone at the department—"

"Is deliberately trying to get me fired," she finished. "I know." Drawing a shaky breath, she forced a smile. "I had a hard time believing it myself, but there's no other explanation. I know I didn't mess up those reports, Carl, and this is the only answer I could come up with.''

He shook his head slowly, obviously thinking about what she'd just told him. ''Have you gone to the chief?''

''No.'' She shook her head quickly. ''It's almost impossible at this point to prove anything. You know how he was about Jerome Lessing. He told me I couldn't blame sloppy police work on another officer. I need proof. I need to find out who is doing this. And I could use your help.''

''My help?''

''I have to be able to trust someone,'' Finn said. ''And have someone looking out for me on that level—someone everyone else trusts, too.''

''Do you have any idea who it might be?''

''No. That's why it's so tough. Some of the guys don't seem to have a lot of respect for me, but no one has been malicious.'' Finn almost hated to ask the next question. ''Do you have any ideas?''

''Wes always calls you the Meter Maid,'' Carl said in an offhand manner. ''But that doesn't mean anything. Everyone knows he's a chauvinist. He admits it himself.''

Finn had had no idea she had a nickname and the knowledge stung, although she didn't let Carl see how it affected her. ''You'll help me?''

''I'll keep my eyes and ears open from now on,'' Carl promised. ''You did the right thing telling me, Finn, but don't let anyone else know. We'll get this figured out.''

She smiled. ''Thanks, Carl.''

She dropped him off at home and went back to the department for briefing.

Gil was at the dispatch center and he nodded briefly when she walked in. "Kelly."

"Hi, Gil." She checked her box and then went to the back table to scan through the reports from the previous shift. There wasn't a lot going on except that they were coming up to the Fourth of July holiday, which meant an influx of people at the parks and more traffic through the area.

Her shift was almost ending when Gil's voice came over the radio. Apparently a group of young people had started breaking bottles against the side of the high school to liven up things.

"Ten-four," Finn said into the radio. "871 responding."

The minute she turned the squad car into the parking lot, several of the teens scattered. The rest stood tensely as Finn got out of the car and walked toward them.

"Officer Kelly!" a voice hailed her cheerfully.

Ricky Calhoun.

He sauntered up to her, a slim blond girl tucked under his arm. "How's it going?"

"I got a vandalism complaint a few minutes ago," Finn said.

"Vandalism?" Ricky grinned and his bravado seemed to ignite the confidence of the others standing nearby. "Anybody here know anything about vandalism?"

Two of the boys laughed and shook their heads. Finn wondered if they would be so arrogant if it were Wes they were facing. Or Carl. Or any of the other male officers.

"Those bottles were broken before we got here," Ricky said. "Weren't they, Lori?"

The blonde's head bobbed up and down in agreement.

"We have a description," Finn said. "Someone saw you."

"Send the bill to my old man." Ricky shrugged, turning to walk away.

"You'll have to come down to the station. I'm arresting the three of you for disorderly conduct and damage to property." Finn had a sudden thought. If she could get Ricky Calhoun fingerprinted, he might be implicated in the string of fires that the community had suffered. Because he had been a juvenile the first time he'd gotten into trouble, he hadn't had his prints taken.

Ricky stared at her in amazement. The girl shifted nervously under his arm.

"Ricky?" she said plaintively.

"I didn't do anything!" One of the younger boys spoke up. "It was Ricky."

"Shut up!" Ricky said rudely.

"Okay, Ricky, hands behind your back," Finn said and pulled the handcuffs out of the holder on her belt. She snapped them on his wrists. "Get in the squad car."

Fleetingly, she wondered why Wes hadn't shown up to see if she needed help. She had heard him check out on a traffic stop just before she reached the school, but surely he would have finished up and swung by to see if she needed assistance.

"You're making a big mistake," Ricky sneered as they drove away. He crossed his arms sullenly and stared out the window.

She took him back to the department where the first

person she saw was Wes, standing in the dispatch area and holding a can of soda.

"Kelly." The older officer's eyes narrowed as he recognized Ricky Calhoun.

"He was breaking bottles against the high school."

"I told her I didn't do it," Ricky said disdainfully, "but she won't believe me."

"You're arresting him?" Wes asked.

"That's right."

"You've got a witness?"

Finn was beginning to wonder why Wes was so interested, but she nodded. "A citizen who was driving by saw them."

"Maybe this time you would just agree to clean up the bottles?" Wes turned to Ricky.

Finn froze. "Wes…"

"Instead of a two-hundred-and-sixty-dollar fine," he added.

"Sure, Officer. Not that I'm saying I did it, but I can do my civic duty by keeping the town clean." He smirked at Finn.

Finn couldn't believe Wes was just going to let the youth go. Especially after she had made the decision to arrest him. She wanted to get Ricky's fingerprints.

"I knew you would," Wes said approvingly. "And Officer Kelly will watch you to make sure you do a good job."

Almost shaking with the force of her emotions, Finn escorted Ricky back to the school grounds and stood for over an hour while he halfheartedly cleaned up the glass. Occasionally, he would leer at her, but outwardly she didn't let him see how upset she was by the whole situation.

Back at the station, she found Wes in the break room

and decided to confront him. "Do you think that letting Ricky get away with vandalism just because his last name happens to be Calhoun was a good idea?"

Wes's eyebrows dipped together at her tone. "Lighten up, Kelly. He didn't get away with anything. He had to clean it up, didn't he?"

"It was a joke to him," Finn said. "Maybe an arrest and a fine, instead of just the threat of a fine, would have made more of an impact."

"The only thing it would have impacted would have been your personnel file," Wes shot back at her. "There is a little thing called *politics* that you need to acquaint yourself with if you're going to be here for the long haul."

"No one is above the law," Finn maintained. "Not the Calhouns, not anyone."

Wes shook his head. "Sorry, Finn, that's not the way the world works."

His words still echoed in her mind when she lay in bed that night. Maybe it was Wes who was trying to get her fired. Maybe that was part of his personal brand of *politics*. The Meter Maid. She suddenly remembered Carl mentioning that was Wes's nickname for her. His lack of respect had certainly crossed the line from break room banter to challenging her authority as an officer. And Ricky Calhoun knew it. It had been evident in his smug expression even when he was cleaning up the broken glass.

Lord, bring these things that are in the darkness out into the light. I need Your help!

The next afternoon when Finn started her shift, the first thing she learned was that another storage shed, this one close to the school, had burned down during the night. She could have cried with frustration. Maybe it was time to go to the chief with her suspicions about who had been setting the fires in Miranda Station. On the other hand, Wes had let Ricky Calhoun walk away from an act of vandalism without so much as a slap on the wrist. Carl had been right. She was going to have to have something concrete on Calhoun before the chief would take her hunch seriously.

The rest of the week passed uneventfully. Off duty for several days, she busily helped her grandparents get ready for the wave of Kellys that would be descending upon them on Friday. Several times when the telephone rang, she hoped to hear John Gabriel's voice, but it was always someone else.

Don't think about him, Finn. You were just part of an investigation. Just another case. Like Chief says, he's a loner. He probably hasn't given you a single thought since you left Chicago.

As stern as she was about trying to control her wayward thoughts about John, there was a loneliness inside that she hadn't experienced before she met him.

Chapter Twelve

Despite the fact that there were probably close to fifty people milling around in Seamus and Anne Kelly's backyard, John spotted Finn immediately. She was sitting on a blanket under a tree, surrounded by an adoring segment of the preschool set. Her auburn hair was pulled up into a high ponytail and she was wearing a pair of denim shorts and a blue T-shirt.

A week. That's how long it had been since he had seen her. Now he was beginning to question why he had come back. Why hadn't he just sent for his things? He paused, ready to disappear from view and pretend he'd never come. Too late. She had spotted him. He could tell because she stopped giggling with the children and stared in his direction until there was a collective clamor for her attention. So much for a quick, anonymous escape.

Several of the children scampered off, and Finn rose slowly to her feet as he approached.

"John."

"The plant is still alive," he said by way of a greeting. To his amazement, her cheeks flushed with guilty color.

"Good."

All the children had scurried away except for the two who pressed shyly against Finn and now gazed at him with open curiosity. One was a boy about seven, the other a girl he guessed to be about three or four.

"Maureen and Ben, this is Mr. Gabriel. He's a friend of mine."

John wasn't sure how to talk to children because he wasn't around them very often. Finn seemed to talk to them like she'd talk to anyone else. "You like children," he observed.

"I suppose you eat them for breakfast."

"Actually, they make a better afternoon snack."

"Ouch," Maureen said, pointing to the scar on his face.

"Not anymore," John told her.

"Finn said that's your badge of courage," Ben said suddenly, studying him.

John glanced at Finn, but she ignored him. "Is that so?"

"I have one, too," Ben lifted his arm and showed John an inch-long scratch on his elbow. "Maureen was running down to the road and I fell when I grabbed her."

"That was very brave," Finn said solemnly, with a meaningful look at John.

"Very," he agreed.

"Ouch," Maureen said again, this time pointing to his arm.

"Finn says everyone has pieces missing," Ben said, as if reciting a lesson from memory. "It's God who makes people whole."

"Pieces missing?" John murmured. His eyes scanned her slender frame. "Funny, I don't see any."

"Well, you can't see on the inside, can you?" Finn asked, avoiding his gaze. She looked down at Ben and Maureen. "I think that Ryan is cutting the watermelon now. Shall we get in line?"

"You have an interesting way of looking at the world," John said, falling into step beside her.

"Thank you." Her chin lifted slightly.

"So are you the resident baby-sitter?" he asked.

"No, they just want to be with me."

"I'm surprised you don't have a halo of bluebirds flying around your head," John muttered.

"I don't understand."

"No, I suppose you don't." John tried not to smile. "So what did you want to be when you grew up? A day-care worker? A mommy?"

"A teacher."

There was a moment of silence. "I thought you wanted to be a cop."

Finn stumbled slightly. "I did...I do... That was before."

"Before your brother's accident?"

"Are you still doing an investigation on me, Agent Gabriel?" Finn asked breathlessly. "I thought you had closed my file."

"As far as I'm concerned the case is still open."

They reached the picnic table, where Ryan was busy slicing an enormous watermelon for the crowd of children who had gathered around him.

"John, good to see you."

"Ryan." John inclined his head.

"Finn, over here!" A slender woman waved at them. Finn's mother.

John immediately saw the resemblance. Although her hair was dark brown and threaded with silver, her eyes were that unusual shade of gray and her warm smile was the same. It was easy to see the woman that Finn would become as the years moved forward.

"Mom, this is John Gabriel."

"It's nice to meet you, John," Gillian Kelly said.

"Mrs. Kelly."

"Please, call me Gillian." She slipped an arm around Finn's waist. "Your father was looking for you. He said he checked your gun and you hadn't cleaned it."

Finn almost groaned, aware of the fact that John was looking at her speculatively. It was a game between her and her father, but John wouldn't know that.

"I'll talk to him." Finn turned to John. "Help yourself to some snacks. We're going to be eating supper in a while."

"I'll tag along with you," John said.

Finn wondered about the wary look in his eyes, but she accepted his presence. Actually, she couldn't believe he had shown up at all. She remembered his reaction when she told him about the huge family reunion they had every Fourth of July, and yet this was the day he had chosen to come back.

She discovered her father sitting at the kitchen table with her gun in pieces in front of him.

"Hi, Dad." She wrapped her arms around his neck and dropped a kiss on his cheek.

"Don't sweet-talk me, young lady," her father growled.

"Dad, this is John Gabriel. I'm sure you remember him."

"Nice to see you again, Gabriel," Nolan said, his

tone changing slightly as he squinted up at John. "I don't think our paths have crossed for a long time."

"No, they haven't," John agreed quietly.

Etiquette satisfied, Nolan's gaze swung sternly back to his daughter. "When was the last time you shot this gun?"

"Last night," Finn admitted. "I went to the range for some practice."

"How many did you hit?"

"About half." Finn slid into a chair next to her father and motioned to John to take another.

That distracted Nolan for a minute. "Half? I would think you'd be doing a little better than that by now. Are you getting out there a few times a week?"

"I've been helping Gran get ready for company." Finn sensed that John was getting angry but she couldn't understand why.

"You have to clean your weapon," he said severely. "Your life may depend upon it."

"I know, but I was tired." Finn smiled at her feeble excuse. "I planned on cleaning it this weekend before my next shift starts."

"I did it for you," Nolan said, just as Finn had guessed he had. "But next time, it better be clean."

"Or she's grounded? Sent to bed without supper?" The terse questions came from John, who had leaned forward in the chair.

Finn saw the dangerous look in John's eyes and the answering sparks in her father's. Quickly, she put her hand over John's on the table. "Dad has a vendetta against dirty weapons."

"And for good reason," Nolan said, scowling at John. "I almost got killed when my gun jammed because I was too tired to clean it after a day at the range.''

''I know.'' Finn started putting the weapon back together. ''To tell you the truth, Dad, I didn't clean it last night because I was hoping you'd do it for me!'' She flashed him a mischievous grin that included John, but he didn't smile in return. ''I'm pretty sure they need you to flip burgers now. I did make sure the spatula was clean.''

''Saucy child, aren't you?'' Nolan asked affectionately. He looked at John speculatively. ''I hope you're staying for the rest of the evening, Gabriel. We'll have a bonfire and fireworks later tonight.''

''And the entire Kelly clan tries to outdo each other with cop stories,'' Finn added, and gave her dad a quick hug. ''Tell Mom we'll be out in a few minutes. I'm just going to put this away.''

After her father left, Finn finished putting the trigger lock on the gun, aware that John was watching her.

''Does he always treat you like that?''

''Like what?'' Finn straightened and looked at him in surprise.

''Like you're still a child.''

''It's not that,'' Finn argued, even as she felt a flash of irritation when she thought about Seamus asking John to come and check out things at the department without consulting her first. Her family did tend to be overprotective at times and it was something she'd accepted as a Kelly trait. You looked out for your own. Still, she had the uneasy feeling that by being so accepting of their concern, she'd allowed them access to areas of her life where she should be making her own decisions.

''Doesn't that bother you?'' John asked.

"Apparently not as much as it bothers you." Finn paused before she tried to explain. "My dad may sound gruff, but it all springs from his concern. That's what I tell myself when it seems like he's crossing a line." *Even though it's probably time for me to start gently pointing out those lines,* Finn thought.

John looked like he was about to say more, but then abruptly changed the subject. "How is everything going at the department?"

"Fine." Finn wondered if she should mention the recent situation with Ricky Calhoun, and decided against it. "Carl Davis is going to help me out. He was glad that I confided in him."

"Anything happening? Reports changed?" John pressed.

"No…" She thought about her conversation with Wes.

John saw something flicker in her eyes and a red flag went up. There was something she wasn't telling him. "Finn?"

"Everything's great," she said, heading for the door. "We better hurry. My cousins are like a wave of locusts. We won't get anything to eat unless we get out there now."

John dropped the subject for the moment but fully intended to bring it up later.

"How is Deborah? Have you seen her lately?" Finn asked.

"Diane is home from the hospital now and they're both doing well, according to Neil."

Maureen toddled up to Finn as they reached the picnic table and lifted her arms. "Up."

"What's all over your face?" Finn pretended to

scold as she swung her up. "That looks like watermelon juice, young lady!"

"Can't eat the seeds," Maureen announced, her cornflower-blue eyes solemn.

"That's right." Finn nuzzled the little girl's ear and smiled as she immediately wriggled to be put down. Finn set her on the grass, but Maureen's intention wasn't to nab another slice of watermelon. "Up."

She looked at John as she said it.

"Pushy little thing, isn't she?" John said over Maureen's head. "It must run in the family."

He bent down and scooped the little girl up. "Happy now?"

Maureen grinned. "War'melon."

"Let's find some," John said, his voice resigned. "You're a lot like your cousin, did you know that? She's bossy, too. She orders trees and pizza without consulting anyone."

"It's not a tree, it's a plant."

"Did you specify how *big* the plant was supposed to be?"

"No," she admitted.

"Well, your plant looks me in the eye whenever I walk over to the window." John leaned over so Maureen could grab a slice of watermelon off the platter.

"Oh, no."

"And it came with a set of instructions as thick as *War and Peace,* too," he grumbled. "Not only do I have to water it, but it also needs to be fertilized, spritzed with warm water once a week and turned occasionally to receive the maximum benefit of the sun."

Finn couldn't prevent the fit of giggles that came over her. "I'm sorry!"

"If I wanted something that high maintenance, I'd have a family," John groused.

Finn's laughter died as quickly as it had sprung up. His green eyes reflected an odd light as she reached for Maureen. "You're forgetting something."

"What is that?"

He looked bored, and Finn felt a stab of hurt. "While you are taking care of your family, they're taking care of you, too."

"Like yours takes care of you?" John asked cynically. "I'm surprised they wanted you in law enforcement at all, considering the danger factor. But at least they managed to pick a nice quiet place for you to work."

"*I* chose this department," Finn said. "Chief just told me there was a job opening here."

She looked confused...and angry. Did she really think that the fact she was a Kelly had nothing to do with getting hired at Miranda Station? She was fresh out of recruit school with no experience. He couldn't believe she was that naive.

"Right." John backed off slightly. It was up to Seamus to tell her the truth about her job.

"My mama." Maureen suddenly began to struggle in Finn's arms as a young woman approached them. She was obviously from the Kelly side of the family. Her trademark auburn hair was whisked back into a casual braid and her smile encompassed them all.

"Gran needs you in the kitchen, Finn."

Finn was thankful for the disruption. "I'm on my way. John, this is my cousin Kathleen."

"A right proper Irish name," the woman laughed, her voice taking on a lilting Irish accent. "If you're born into the Kelly family, you get an Irish name. 'Tis a grand tradition!''

''It's nice to meet you, Kathleen.''

Finn made her escape as Kathleen drew him into conversation. She was only four years older than Finn but had married right out of high school. Her father, Finn's uncle, was a detective, and one evening he'd brought home a young man who was studying police photography. Fourteen months later, he and Kathleen were married. Finn had been one of her bridesmaids.

When Finn entered the kitchen, she was immediately laden down with two large bowls of potato salad to take outside. She looked for John and saw him talking to her father and Seamus near the grill. What had he meant when he said that they had picked out a quiet place for her to work? That Chief had been instrumental in getting her the job at Miranda Station? The thought was troubling. She knew she had the qualifications necessary for being hired. She had ranked second in her class at recruit school. John must have assumed that Chief had used his friendship with Chief Larson to get her a job. That was the only explanation.

John couldn't deny one thing—the Kelly family knew how to have fun. An afternoon of swimming, games and food melted into an evening with a bonfire, more games and more food. Finn had steered clear of him most of the afternoon, but when the children were settled sleepily into their parents' laps by the fire, she came and sat with him and Ryan.

Then the stories began, just as she had claimed they would. For over an hour, the law enforcement members of the family traded stories back and forth. John noticed that Finn remained quiet and Ryan had a pensive look on his face. Suddenly, he realized that Finn had positioned her body directly in front of him and her brother on the grass, creating an almost protective barrier between them and the rest of the group. Just as the realization struck, he discovered why.

Nolan Kelly's voice boomed out suddenly. "I'm sure John Gabriel has a few stories to share."

John felt everyone's eyes on him and he forced a smile.

"Well, Dad, he could tell us, but then he'd have to kill us, wouldn't he?" Finn teased.

Laughter erupted from the group but they still leaned forward eagerly to hear what he would add.

"I doubt my stories are as interesting as yours," John said.

"Not interesting? A Madison Agent?" one of the teenage boys scoffed. "You probably see more action in a week than my dad does in a year!"

Finn turned and looked at him. "Do you want some help getting out of this one, Agent Gabriel, or would you rather go it alone?"

"Some help would be appreciated, thank you."

Finn rose to her feet. "You'll have to catch him tomorrow, folks. John promised to go for a walk with me."

There was a murmur of surprise, but Nolan gave in. "All right, but there's no getting out of it later, Gabriel."

As they left the warmth of the bonfire, Finn shivered, suddenly chilly in her T-shirt and shorts. "I'm going back home to get a sweatshirt."

"You just gave them something else to talk about," John said abruptly as they reached her house.

Finn opened the door and he followed her inside. "What do you mean?"

"You made it look like we were together." How innocent was she, anyway? He'd seen the smiles on their faces. The knowing looks.

"I did not." Finn seemed indignant. "I just said we were going for a walk."

"In the dark. Just the two of us."

For a second it appeared she was prepared to argue the point. "Oh."

"Right." John felt a ripple of anger but wasn't sure why.

"I didn't mean to…" She hesitated as she searched his eyes. "You're angry."

She couldn't even discern anger from desire. He pulled her against him, hearing the soft gasp that escaped from her lips. "Not angry, Finn," he muttered, and kissed her. It should have been awkward, holding a woman. But it wasn't. At least, not Finn. Maybe he had started out angry but just the touch of her lips sent that particular emotion running in the opposite direction. The amazing thing was, she was kissing him back. With no awkwardness, no hesitation, Finn melted against him and traced the contour of his back with her fingers. He breathed in the scent that was uniquely her, and for a split second, he recognized the beauty of the moment. This was something he had wanted to do from the day he'd met her. What stunned him was the possibility that maybe she felt the same way.

And this was an added complication he didn't need in his life. He broke their embrace as quickly as he'd started it. She stumbled against him, as if her legs weren't quite steady. Without thinking, he reached out his hand to steady her and let his fingers drift down her arm. He was a second away from pulling her against him again… Silently calling himself a fool, he broke the contact with her and stepped away.

"John…"

"Finn, this was a mistake. You know it as well as I do."

She didn't deny it, and he felt a painful stab in the vicinity of his heart.

"Are we still going to go for a walk?" she asked, her voice a little shaky.

"I think you already know the answer to that." The temptation to spend more time with her was crashing over him. "I'll see you in the morning."

Chapter Thirteen

The next morning, Finn found her father and Seamus on the patio sharing a pot of coffee. Most of the family was still sleeping, although the silence was punctuated by some of the babies beginning to fuss for their breakfast.

"Morning, sweetheart."

"Hi, Dad, Chief." Finn pulled up a redwood chair and sat down. "Did you two have any influence in getting me hired here?"

The moment of silence told her the truth. Her father cleared his throat and glanced at Seamus.

"You were perfectly qualified for the job, Finn," Seamus sputtered.

"That's not what I asked."

"Oh, you're taking it too seriously," Nolan said, obviously uncomfortable. "It happens all the time. Someone puts in a good word, that's all there is to it. You're proving yourself."

"I may not make my probation."

''What!'' As one, Seamus and Nolan voiced the word.

Matter-of-factly, Finn told them what had been going on for the past few months.

''I'll go in and talk to Larson myself—'' Seamus began, but Finn quickly cut him off.

''No, Chief. I've already got Carl Davis working on it with me. If I don't have any proof that someone's trying to sabotage my job, it's only going to look worse to Larson.''

Nolan was nodding. ''She's right, Da.''

''I'd like to get my hands on whoever is trying to make you look bad,'' Seamus muttered, ''but I'll stay out of it, Finn, if that's what you want.''

It was obvious from the unhappy expression on her grandfather's face that was not what *he* wanted.

''And you can call off your other investigation, too.''

Seamus scowled and Nolan looked perplexed.

''Investigation?''

''John Gabriel.'' Finn felt a stab of emotion as she said his name but resolutely pushed it away. ''Chief hired him to check up on me.''

''I didn't hire the man.'' Seamus blustered a denial. ''He did it as a favor…oh, all right. I'll talk to him.''

''We're just looking out for you, sweetheart,'' Nolan said in his father's defense.

Finn summoned a smile. ''I realize that, Dad, but I'm a grown woman.''

She didn't miss the quick glance they exchanged. Apparently, they didn't believe her! John had been right all along.

''I'm not a little girl you need to take care of,'' Finn said, frustration bubbling up inside of her. ''I love the fact that we're a close family but that doesn't mean you live my life for me, make decisions that I should be making. *Or,*—'' she tossed a meaningful glance at Seamus but took his hand to soften the sting of her words ''—go all cloak-and-dagger on me and make a call for reinforcements.''

Nolan shifted uncomfortably. ''I think that's a bit harsh, Finn. You don't have a husband to look out for you yet…''

Finn didn't hear the rest of the sentence because she saw Chief's face redden and a thought struck her. *What if…*

No, he wouldn't have. That was impossible. Impossible.

''I'm going to take Colin for a walk.'' She needed some time to clear the cobwebs from her brain. Time to pray.

The way the evening before had ended, she wouldn't have been surprised to learn that John had simply packed up his things and disappeared during the night. She almost hoped he had. She had little experience with men and none whatsoever with men of his caliber. He was too complex. Too bitter. The attraction she felt for him was confusing—and frustrating. Yet, last night he had shown it was a mutual attraction. At least, she amended, on the physical side. It didn't mean he wanted to take her out for dinner. Or spend the rest of his life with her.

His comments on marriage had definitely been negative.

Marriage.

Finn stopped running and stood in the middle of the sidewalk for a moment, vaguely aware that her side had cramped. *What are you thinking about?* she scolded herself. *You act like you're in love with him.*

"Finn!"

She turned and saw Kathleen.

"If I had known you were going to go for a run, I would have been up earlier." Kathleen covered the distance between them easily, but when she saw Finn's expression, her smile faded. "What's the matter?"

"Nothing." Finn tried to smile back but failed miserably.

Kathleen linked her arm through Finn's and they fell into step together. "This wouldn't have anything to do with John Gabriel, would it?"

Finn groaned. "Is it that obvious?"

Kathleen laughed. "I recognize the signs."

"It's confusing."

"He couldn't keep his eyes off you last night," Kathleen said. "Does that help?"

Finn's heart pounded as she heard the words. "That doesn't mean anything, does it, Kat?"

"No," Kathleen said truthfully. "Not always. Not if you're looking for something deeper."

"I can't." Finn turned troubled eyes on her cousin. "But I've been praying for him since we met a few weeks ago. He probably wouldn't describe himself as a believer, but he's at the starting point—if he didn't believe in God, he wouldn't be so angry with Him."

"He seems like a hard man, Finn," Kathleen admitted. "The kind of person you're glad is on the right side of the law."

Finn knew what she meant. He had a dangerous quality about him. Her thoughts suddenly swept her back to the hospital room where John had held the Averys' baby. She had seen the mixture of awe and tenderness skim across his features before the familiar walls were resurrected. There was more to John Gabriel than he let people see. Much more.

"Did he leave yet?"

"No, and it didn't look like he was packing his suitcase, either," Kathleen said. "Sorry to disappoint you. When I left to catch up with you, he was talking to Chief and your dad."

"I suppose we better get back soon." Finn sighed. Who knew what Seamus was plotting now!

Kathleen nudged her. "Try to smile. Men expect women to look miserable when they're in love!"

In love. That wasn't possible. And Finn knew that John didn't "expect" anything from her.

Finn decided to give up her daily run in exchange for a leisurely walk around the neighborhood with Kathleen. When they returned, signs of life were abundant. The children were in the yard, playing with an enormous beach ball while their parents sat in lawn chairs, sipping coffee.

John watched Finn and Kathleen return through veiled eyes. He had just spent half an hour getting upbraided by Seamus for "blowing his cover" while Nolan Kelly watched in silent approval.

"I can't believe you actually told Finn what you were about," Seamus had blustered. "I thought agents were supposed to be discreet."

"Someone's playing a game with her," John had snapped. "And she's been allowing it to happen for months. I told her to go on the offensive from now on. If I hadn't pushed, hadn't told her why I was here, I wouldn't have gotten anything out of her. I went with my instincts. She's an honest person. You approach her honestly and she responds." There was anger lacing his voice because Seamus and Nolan were related to Finn, her closest family, and yet they didn't seem to know that. He had known her for less than a month and had figured it out. She didn't have a deceitful bone in her body.

"You're right about that." Nolan finally voiced an opinion. "The girl can't lie to save her life. Never could."

"I'm still not convinced she wants to be a cop, Chief." John decided to go for broke. "I think that may factor into the situation."

"Of course she wants to be a cop," Nolan said irritably. "That's what she is, isn't she?"

"Maybe because when a person has the name Kelly they think they don't have a choice," John said steadily.

"Now wait a second..." Nolan rose from his chair, but John didn't back down.

"Doesn't anyone but me think it's a strange coincidence that Finn told you she was going into law enforcement when Ryan wasn't able to?" John's frustration rose as he pictured Finn walking beside him yesterday, inadvertently telling him she had wanted to be a teacher. "Your family ties are strangling her, if you ask me."

"I don't remember asking you!" Nolan said, obviously trying to keep his voice from carrying to the others scattered around the yard. "You—a stranger—presume to tell me about my daughter!"

"It's all right, Nolan," Seamus said. "John may have a point."

Nolan sat down once again, his posture rigid. "I think I know my own child."

"That may be true, but do you know the woman she's become?"

The silence that fell over the men was broken by several of the children scampering up to Seamus and coercing him over to the swimming pool. After an awkward pause, Nolan muttered an excuse and left John alone at the table. That was when he saw Finn and Kathleen returning. As they reached the yard, Finn veered toward her own home while Colin was surrounded by a group of the children, one of whom was holding a Frisbee riddled with canine teeth marks.

John closed his eyes, wondering why he was still here. His suitcase was sitting by the door in the spare room, packed and ready. After last night, Finn had probably expected he would be gone this morning. He could still feel her against him. The tremor that had ripped through her had said it all. She was totally inexperienced. He had guessed it, but now he knew it was true. He wouldn't be surprised to learn that he was the first man who had kissed her. Impossible though it seemed, considering the times they lived in. Yet for a few seconds, she had kissed him back. Until his sanity had returned.

"Finn." Maureen was at his elbow. A bouquet of wilted, damp dandelions was clutched in her hand and yellow pollen dusted her nose.

"She's at home." John pointed to the little house in the distance.

"Come on." Maureen tugged on his arm. "I picked flowers for her."

"You better take them over."

Maureen stared up at him patiently. With a sigh, John rose to his feet.

"Fine. We'll go over there together."

"Up." Maureen lifted her arms and John knelt down, then hoisted her up with his arm. The dandelions brushed his cheek.

When they reached Finn's door, it opened before John could knock. Apparently, she had seen them coming.

"Dan'lions." Maureen thrust the flowers toward Finn, who grinned and took not only the bouquet offered but the child as well.

"They're lovely," Finn said. "Let's put them in some water."

Maureen nodded happily, and John turned to go.

"You, too." Maureen had seen him about to slip away.

Finn paused. Her heart had started to pound erratically again at the sight of him. Why hadn't he left? He looked disturbingly attractive. A faint shadow of stubble testified to the fact he hadn't taken time to shave yet. It enhanced that edge she could sense below the surface. He was dressed casually in blue jeans and a grey cotton shirt, the sleeve neatly pinned.

"Why don't you have an artificial arm?" she asked, voicing the question she had wondered about since they'd met.

"It's been discussed."

Finn frowned. "Discussed by who? Isn't that your decision?" She set Maureen down and immediately the little girl scurried toward the kitchen to find some water for her flowers.

"When I'm on a case people tend to overlook me. A one-armed man couldn't possibly be a threat. Couldn't possibly be a cop. I decided it was actually a benefit."

Finn picked up the thread of cynicism in his tone. "I don't know how anyone could overlook you," she said frankly.

Once again he was totally taken aback. She had a genius for knocking him off center. "I'll take that as a compliment."

"Don't," she said, following Maureen to the kitchen.

John felt himself smile. "All right."

"Here, sweetie." Finn found a small crystal vase in the cupboard and carefully pushed each limp dandelion stem into it while Maureen watched. "Go ahead and put them right on the table."

"Pretty," Maureen declared, studying the arrangement.

"Very pretty." Finn washed her hands and glanced at John. He was staring at her with an unreadable expression in his eyes. "What?"

John couldn't speak. The anger that brewed inside would have erupted had he opened his mouth. Watching her interact with children, it was easy to see she was a natural. She should be sharpening pencils for some first-grade class somewhere or reading picture books to spellbound kindergarteners. And maybe she would be—if her last name wasn't Kelly.

Chapter Fourteen

Finn couldn't believe it, but John stayed for her family's entire Fourth of July celebration. He patiently lit sparklers for the children, flipped hamburgers on the grill and even joined in an impromptu game of volleyball.

Finn kept her distance.

"You have feelings for him, don't you."

"Dad!" Finn's heart jumped at the quiet words near her shoulder. "You scared me."

"I shouldn't have. You should never let your guard down." Nolan's smile took the sting out of the words.

"Yes, well, you're not the only one who's told me that."

"John Gabriel?"

"Yup."

"You didn't answer my question."

"I didn't?"

Finn was sitting on a quilt spread out on the grass, and Nolan dropped down next to her. "Watch your heart with him, honey. I'm not sure he knows what to do with one.''

Finn drew a ragged breath. Just that morning, she had read a verse that cut right to her soul. ''Guard your heart, for it is the wellspring of life.''

''First Kathleen and now you,'' Finn complained. ''The next thing I know, Maureen will be lecturing me.''

''Your mother and I have to go back home tomorrow. You'll let us know if you need anything, won't you?''

Finn detected a note of uncertainty in his voice. ''Sure.''

''John Gabriel thinks you don't want to be a police officer.''

''He told you that?'' Finn asked in astonishment.

''In no uncertain terms,'' Nolan said, his expression making Finn wonder what else they had talked about. ''Don't worry, though, I set him straight. I mean, if you hadn't wanted to go into police work, you would have said something, right? You'll be fine in Miranda Station. It's a nice small department in a quiet town.''

''And that was why Chief put in a good word for me, wasn't it,'' Finn said. ''Because I could be what you wanted in the safest place possible.''

Nolan frowned. ''Gabriel's put ideas into your head. You were thrilled when you graduated second in your class. I could see the pride on your face when you sent us the picture Anne took of you in your new uniform.''

She *had* been thrilled. And proud. Finn couldn't deny it. But more important, she'd wanted *him* to be thrilled. *Him* to be proud. She'd somehow sensed all along that by being born a girl she'd been a disappointment to him. He'd been the one who'd stripped the very feminine name of Fiona down to a masculine nickname. She'd wanted her father and Ryan's relationship to be fixed, but deep inside, she'd also craved Nolan's attention. And approval. There had been a subtle shift when she'd announced she was going to be a cop—a change in the way he treated her. Finn wondered if he was even aware of that.

"Have you talked to Ryan?" Finn asked.

"Ryan?" Nolan frowned. "About what?"

"About anything, Dad," Finn said. "About seminary. About his work at The Wild Olive."

Nolan was silent for a few minutes. "No."

For the first time, Finn felt frustrated with her father. "It's not always about cops and robbers, Dad. Some of the Kellys aren't in law enforcement, but it doesn't mean that what they do is any less important."

"I never said that." Nolan sounded defensive. "Ryan and I—you just don't understand, Finn."

"He thinks he's a disappointment to you." She had wanted to protect Ryan from their father's disappointment. But it hadn't worked. There was still an invisible rift between them.

Nolan's eyes closed briefly. "He said that?"

"He doesn't have to. You sat down with cousin Daniel yesterday and picked his brains about the academy, but I haven't heard you ask Ryan anything about the things he's doing with the shelter."

"I don't understand his—or your—faith," Nolan admitted uncomfortably. "I don't pretend to, Finn. We Kellys have always stood on our own two feet."

Finn squeezed his hand. "Just talk to him." She rose to her feet and stretched, just as a squad car pulled into the driveway. "Looks like Carl wants to tell me something. I'll be back in a minute."

She jogged over to the car and slid into the passenger side. "Don't tell me I'm getting my vacation taken away?"

Carl shook his head. "Just wanted to tell you that they've switched you to afternoon shift tomorrow, that's all."

"How about a glass of lemonade and a really thick fudge brownie while you run radar?" Finn asked.

"Sounds good to me. The air conditioner in here can't keep up today," Carl said, pulling at the collar of his shirt.

"Be right back." When Finn turned, she almost bumped into John, who'd come up behind her. Avoiding his gaze, she ducked her chin and sprinted across the lawn.

"She runs like a girl," Carl commented with a chuckle.

"Don't they all," John said. "You got stuck working the holiday?"

"I don't mind." Carl stifled a yawn. "It's just another day. Only this one gets overtime."

It wasn't just another day to the Kellys, John thought briefly. "Planning to go to the fireworks with your family tonight?"

"No." Carl shook his head. "My wife is out of town this weekend on business."

Something in his voice gave John pause. He leaned casually against the door of the squad. "What does she do?"

"She's big into this up-and-coming art studio," Carl said. "I'm lucky if I can get a decent meal these days. You know how it is. She breezes in at seven o'clock and acts surprised that I don't have dinner on the table.

It used to be steak and mashed potatoes. Now most of the time it's takeout.''

"I'm single," John threw in.

"Lucky guy," Carl muttered. "At least you've never come to expect hot meals and clean shirts."

"No." John's lips twisted slightly. "I don't expect it."

"She says it's *her turn*. Whatever that means! I guess it means it's her turn and forget about me."

John saw Finn coming back toward them with a huge glass of lemonade. Carl grinned and pushed his mirrored sunglasses back on his nose.

"Just what the doctor ordered," he said.

"How's Sherilynn?" Finn asked, handing him the glass.

Carl took a long drink and smacked his lips appreciatively. "Couldn't be better. Well, duty calls. Oh, I almost forgot to tell you. A bunch of us from work are getting together at Reilly's tonight. If you're free, stop in." He saluted briefly and drove away.

"Reilly's?"

"It's a restaurant outside town," Finn explained as he fell in step with her. "The guys go there a lot."

"And you don't."

"I guess I'm not very comfortable in that setting." She shrugged.

"It might make you more a part of the group."

"Or less a part." She couldn't explain to him how she had felt the one and only time she had shown up at Reilly's. It had been shortly after she'd been hired, and Wes had spent the hour she was there cracking "blonde" jokes, the rest of the guys laughing in proportion to the number of drinks they'd had. She had decided on the way home that night that she wouldn't go to Reilly's just to "fit in." There would be other opportunities to get to know them.

John got to Reilly's at eight that night. It was a mom-and-pop place, with lumpy red vinyl booths and plastic ivy hanging in baskets from the ceiling. In a nod to technology, however, there was a newly purchased big-screen TV set up in one corner. The officers took up most of the dining area. They had pushed together several tables in the center and were laughing uproariously about something when John walked over.

"John Gabriel!" Carl raised a hand when he spotted them.

"Hope you don't mind my crashing your get-together. Too many kids at the Kelly reunion. I decided I needed some adult conversation."

A chair scraped against the floor as one of the guys pulled it away from the table. "Are you kidding? Sit down!"

"Finn coming?" Carl asked.

"She said I should take her place," John said casually. "I don't think she wanted her innocent ears burned."

There was a sudden silence as everyone assessed his comment. John leaned back in the chair and dipped a handful of pretzels out of the wicker basket in front of him. "To be honest, I'd hate to have my life depend on her. She needs help weeding the garden." He signaled for a waitress.

"Thought you were thick with the old man," Wes said, his eyes narrow.

"We go back," John said, "but I couldn't believe it when he told me his granddaughter was a cop, too. Probably went into law enforcement to get a husband."

"It wouldn't be the first time," one of the guys said. There was a ripple of laughter and the men relaxed.

"Well, Alloway is the only single guy on the force." Carl grinned at the young man sitting beside him.

"Ah, fifty bucks says she won't make probation." Wes growled the words and tossed back his drink.

"Hey, I was her training officer!" Carl pretended to be insulted. "Everyone I train makes his probation."

"Right, you said it. *His* probation. We're not talking about a him, though. We're talking about a her."

Wes rolled his eyes. "It's got nothing to do with training."

John tilted his head, regarding the man with interest. "No?"

"She's got everything she needs to be a cop except one thing," Wes said. "A thick skin."

Some of the others murmured in agreement.

"After she took Jerome Lessing to jail, I found her crying in the break room," Wes said disdainfully.

"Soft," Keith Parachek interjected.

For the next hour, John listened. He listened to their marital problems. He listened while they talked shop. He heard their gripes. And boasts. They talked freely in front of him, collectively, silently, knowing he was *one* of them. It was apparent that Wes and Carl were at the top of the pecking order and the others seemed to follow their lead. What disturbed him was that none of them had shown any loyalty to Finn. Granted, not all the officers on the Miranda Station police force were at Reilly's that night, but if he were a betting man, he'd have to say the sentiment was probably the same.

He drove back to Seamus's later that night. Somewhere in the distance, he could hear the staccato sound of fire crackers. By morning, the cars that lined the street and filled the driveway would be gone. And so would he. There was nothing to keep him here anymore. Finn had help at the department to discover who was trying to get her fired…

Then why couldn't he get over the nagging feeling that he was missing something? As he walked toward the house, he replayed the conversations he had listened to throughout the evening. Wes was his obvious choice, but he wore his prejudices like a banner and he hadn't once hinted that he had anything against Finn as an officer because she was a woman. It was the woman she *was* that seemed to rub him the wrong way.

A soft ripple of laughter and quiet voices drew his attention suddenly. Some of the Kellys were obviously still enjoying the celebration with a late-night swim. He could hear the gentle slap of the water against the concrete as he drew closer.

"The Wild Olive has asked me to be their director." Ryan's voice carried clearly through the darkness.

"Ryan! Have you told Mom and Dad?"

John closed his eyes. *Finn.*

"I think Dad might be more interested if they had asked me to be their security guard," Ryan said, his attempt at humor falling flat. There was no mistaking the discouragement in his voice.

"Are you going to accept?"

"I'm still praying about it," Ryan said. "I always figured that when I graduated from seminary, I'd have a church. You know, be a pastor."

"Oh, sure," Finn said. "The pastor of a building!"

Ryan laughed. "You cut to the chase, don't you, little sister. The truth is, The Wild Olive struggles for every penny it has. I don't see much change in the lives of the people we work with and the pay would keep me in the poverty to which I've become accustomed.''

''Well, you're not working for The Wild Olive, are you?'' Finn asked reasonably. ''You're working for God. He owns the cattle on a thousand hills, He's the one who changes people's lives and He has a great retirement plan. I guess I can see what you're worried about.''

Ryan groaned. ''*You* should be the preacher!''

John could almost feel Finn smile in the darkness. ''Well, I've learned from the best.''

''Then you won't mind if I turn the tables on you,'' Ryan said. ''If I get to take over as the director, then that leaves my position open.''

There was a moment of silence.

''I think I'd make a better security guard.'' Finn laughed shakily. ''It's what I'm trained to do.''

''You love people, you love to make a difference…this is a *ministry* opportunity, Finn, not just a job! And, Finn, I've been wondering lately if maybe you never felt like you had a choice about going into law enforcement. Because of what happened to me?''

''Every job is a ministry opportunity,'' Finn reminded him, skirting around his other questions. ''I think you told me that.''

''There you go again, making me live my own words.'' Ryan chuckled. ''Will you at least promise to pray about it, Finn?''

''You know I will.''

''Actually, I thought the idea of moving to Chicago might appeal to you for another reason.''

''What's that?''

''John Gabriel.''

The name hung silently in the darkness between

them. John caught his breath, suddenly very aware that he was eavesdropping on a private conversation. Because of his job, it was second nature to him to pick up information by any means.

"Yes, well—" Finn drew in a ragged breath. "Remember that tree house we made when we were kids? The one out of boards and rope?"

"You were scared to death of that thing," Ryan remembered with a chuckle.

"I know. And John Gabriel reminds me of that tree house."

And that, John thought, was another reason to leave the next morning and not look back.

Chapter Fifteen

Finn had a hollow feeling inside the next morning as the cars, loaded with Kellys, drove away, hands fluttering goodbyes behind the sun-streaked windows. Seamus looked tired, his arm circling Anne's waist as they watched the last family leave.

Finn shaded her eyes against the sun with one hand and waved to Maureen with the other as the blue van pulled away.

"'Bye, Auntie Finn!" The childish voice drifted through the open window, and Finn smiled.

"It's always so quiet when everyone leaves," Anne said pensively. "And you have to work this afternoon, don't you, Finn?"

"Two until ten," Finn said. "I'll help with the cleanup, though, Gran."

"There is no cleanup, sweetheart," Anne said. "Everyone pitched in this morning and it's all done. I think your grandpa and I are just going to soak up some sun this afternoon beside the pool and play some Scrabble."

''Do you know what happened to John?'' Finn asked. There were some things she wanted to say to him. She had been thinking a lot about the bonfire two nights ago. When Anne told her he hadn't made an appearance yet, Finn cautiously went upstairs and knocked on his door.

''John?'' She hesitated when he opened the door. He looked aloof, almost unapproachable as he met her gaze. ''Chief said you're leaving pretty soon. I've got to leave for work so I thought I'd come up and say goodbye.''

''Goodbye.'' The words were said with cool detachment, and Finn realized they were intended to guarantee a quick retreat from the person on the receiving end of them. Well, she wasn't going to retreat. Not yet, anyway!

''Was there something else?'' His eyebrow rose.

Finn swallowed hard. He definitely wasn't making this easy. ''I just wanted to tell you that I'm sorry for the other night.'' She felt the heat in her face. ''If I did anything to make you think…'' This was more difficult than she had thought.

''That you'd be willing to add another dimension to our relationship?''

His directness drained the color from her face. ''I— Yes.''

''You didn't do anything but stand next to me.''

His callous words struck her to the core. ''I see.''

''Goodbye, Finn.'' He eyed her impassively.

She backed away from the door and walked numbly down the stairs. It was a relief when the squad car finally pulled in the driveway. At least for the next eight hours she could disappear into her job.

*   *   *

John watched from the window as the squad car pulled away. She'd apologized to *him*. He could almost read her thoughts. Maybe she had been out of line. Maybe she'd flirted with him. Maybe her T-shirt was too tight. Maybe she had said something to encourage him.

Why was she so persistent in always thinking she was to blame for everything? He slammed his hand down on the windowsill. He had just insulted her. Basically told her that she wasn't anything special to him, when he was beginning to realize that just the opposite was true. They were as different as night and day. She knew it, too. This unusual attraction that had sprung up between them would fade away. He'd been in the darkness too long and Finn was the light that hurt his eyes.

Seamus convinced him to stay into the afternoon. Anne had fallen asleep in the lawn chair, her straw hat shading her face from the sun, and John had a hunch that the sudden exodus of the family had left Seamus feeling at a loss.

"I must have left my glasses on my nightstand," Seamus said, searching his pockets without success.

"I'll get them for you, then I should get going." John smiled at Seamus's obvious relief at not having to trudge up the stairs to his bedroom, which was on the second floor.

The room was a master bedroom suite, decorated in relaxing shades of ivory and sage. There was an enormous family portrait hanging above the bed, full of redheaded Kellys and a few Donovan dark-haired "throwbacks." He picked out Finn in an instant. She must have been in high school when the photo was taken. Her delicate features and wide gray eyes were a standout among all the others.

Just as he found the eyeglasses and picked them up, the police scanner on Chief's dresser crackled to life.

"871, can you copy? A 10-28 at Idlewild Boulevard."

He waited curiously to see what that code would translate to.

"871, I copy." Finn's voice came back over the radio.

"A neighbor called and reported a couple fighting."

A domestic disturbance.

"Ten-four."

"871? That's the Lessings' residence again."

John knew the name sounded familiar. But why? Tapping his fingers on the top of the nightstand, he replayed his conversations with Finn. Lessing—the one she was supposed to testify against in court. The domestic dispute that had left her crying and Wes scornful of her emotional response.

He glanced at the clock. It looked like he wasn't going back to Chicago just yet.

Finn responded to the call to the Lessing home. She had hoped that Bonnie Lessing hadn't taken her husband back in after he got out of jail. Apparently, she had. Finn hit the siren once to clear the traffic off the street ahead of her.

"871, is 876 on the way for backup?"

"Negative," the dispatcher said. "876 is on a traffic stop."

Finn pulled up in front of the apartment building and heard the cries coming from inside. She couldn't wait for backup, although she knew she was supposed to.

Domestic disputes were the most dangerous situations for a police officer and the department had strict guidelines on policy and procedure. Finn heard Bonnie Lessing scream and decided that policy and procedure were going to have to take a back seat to a woman's safety.

She sprinted up to the house and pounded on the door.

"Police!"

There was a sudden, unnatural silence.

"Police. Open the door."

Bonnie Lessing's daughter opened the door. She was about four years old, with limp brown hair and wide dark eyes. Somehow the fact that Tina was about the same age as Maureen made it worse for Finn.

"Is your mommy here? Can I talk to her?"

The little girl opened the door and stood to the side, two fingers tucked in her mouth.

"Mrs. Lessing? Bonnie?" Finn had one hand on her gun as she walked cautiously into the house. She glanced down. "Do you remember me, Tina? I'm Officer Kelly."

The little girl nodded.

"Tina, I want you to stay behind me. Will you do that?"

She nodded again.

"Is there a problem, Officer?" Jerome Lessing stepped into the room, his hands behind his back.

"Mr. Lessing, I want you to keep your hands where they are and turn around slowly," Finn directed. She heard a moan from the living room. "Mrs. Lessing? Are you all right?"

"She's fine," Jerome said harshly, ignoring her instructions to turn around. "Feeling a little under the weather today, is all."

Tina hung back and pressed against the wall.

"Mr. Lessing, turn around now!" Finn said, more loudly than she had the first time.

"I don't take orders from a woman."

Finn felt a shiver of apprehension. Where in the world was her backup? It was Mike Alloway that was working with her that afternoon, with Wes on duty as the supervisor. She began to pray silently, never taking her eyes off Jerome Lessing.

Bonnie Lessing suddenly appeared in the doorway behind her husband. There were no bruises on her face this time but she was cradling her arm. "I'm okay, Officer Kelly."

"I would like to talk with you in the kitchen, Mrs. Lessing."

"Nothing to talk about," Jerome said. "Those neighbors got nothing better to do than poke their noses where they don't belong."

Bonnie Lessing looked pleadingly at her husband, her eyes dark. "Jerome…"

"Did he hurt you, Mrs. Lessing?"

"He twisted Mommy's arm," Tina said suddenly, flying to Finn's side as her father moved forward threateningly. Bonnie ducked past him and moved quickly to stand by Finn, too.

The unexpected maneuver distracted Jerome, and Finn chose that moment to grab his arm and pull it behind his back, snapping the handcuffs into place. Her fear that he had been holding a weapon was blessedly unfounded.

"Is that true, Mrs. Lessing? Did he hurt you?"

"She had it coming," Jerome said bitterly.

"That's enough, Mr. Lessing," Finn said. "Mrs. Lessing, I'm going to call an ambulance so they can check out your arm. And I'm going to need a statement from you."

For a moment, Bonnie Lessing looked frightened, then she touched the top of Tina's head.

"All right, Officer."

"Is there someone I can call to take care of Tina?"

Bonnie nodded, her face pale. "My sister," she whispered.

"I can take him in, Finn," Alloway said as he appeared in the doorway.

Finn was relieved to see him, though she would have been more relieved if he'd arrived ten minutes earlier.

An hour later, Finn was back at the department, beginning to fill out her report.

"Kelly."

It was Wes.

"You didn't wait for backup at the domestic."

"I couldn't," Finn said. "When I got there, I could hear Bonnie Lessing screaming, Wes. Mike had checked out on a traffic stop." *Where were you,* she wanted to ask.

"Our policy is that no one goes in alone to a domestic dispute," Wes said. "You know that, Finn."

Finn remained silent. She did know that. And she knew the danger she had placed herself in when she entered the house. But she hadn't been able to ignore Bonnie. A few minutes could mean everything to the victim in that type of situation. Bonnie had a broken arm, but if Jerome had had more time, her injuries might have been worse.

"I'm writing you up," Wes said flatly.

"It took Mike almost ten minutes to get there," Finn said, trying to keep her tone calm and reasonable. "Who knows what would have happened to Bonnie Lessing if I'd stayed outside waiting for backup."

"Who knows what could have happened to *you*."

"Nothing happened to me!"

"This time." Wes shook his head. "What about next time?"

She knew better than to continue the argument. It was evident by the expression on Wes's face that he wasn't going to listen. "Where were you?" she asked quietly.

His eyes narrowed. "What do you mean?"

"You knew Mike was on a traffic stop, so why didn't you respond as my backup?"

He stared at her as if he had never seen her before. "I wasn't available either," he finally said.

"I'm sure the chief is going to want to know where you were when you hand in your report," Finn said. "You should probably make sure it's in there."

Wes turned on his heel and strode out of the room. Finn sank against the back of the chair, feeling her hands tremble. Suddenly the thought of working with Ryan at The Wild Olive was very appealing. Doggedly, she finished her report and turned it in to the dispatcher. In spite of Wes's threats, she took satisfaction in knowing that Jerome Lessing was in jail and that Bonnie had, for the first time, agreed to go for counseling at the local domestic abuse shelter.

By the end of her shift, Finn discovered a letter on her desk written in Wes's bold scrawl. He told her to be in to work half an hour earlier the next day to meet with him and Chief Larson. She had never been so relieved to have her shift end and see her house waiting for her, a light in the window welcoming her return.

Before she realized it, the tears started to fall. She was too weary to wipe them away. It wasn't because her job was on the line. Bonnie Lessing's face was imprinted in her mind. The haunted, hopeless look in her eyes. The fear reflected in her daughter's.

She pushed the door open, wondering briefly why Colin hadn't made a fuss. The second she walked inside, she realized why. John was slouched on her sofa, Colin curled up contentedly at his feet.

Hastily, she brushed her hand across her cheeks and blinked away the tears. But she wasn't quick enough. Not that it would have mattered anyway. There were more spilling over even as she made the attempt.

"I thought you went back to Chicago." She grabbed a tissue from the box on the counter and made a few more halfhearted swipes at the damage.

He was silent for a moment. "Seamus wasn't feeling well."

"What? Is he all right? Is he having chest pains again?" *What next, Lord?*

"He's complaining his chest feels a little tight," John admitted. "He thinks it's from all the excitement, but Anne was worried, so I said I'd stay another night." He saw the expression on her face and held up his hand. "Not to worry now. He's asleep. I checked on them before I came over here."

"She should have called me."

"Sounds like you had your hands full."

The police scanner. Finn didn't even have to ask. She dropped into the chair opposite him and absently stroked Colin with the toe of her shoe.

"Why are you crying?"

"Am I?" Finn sighed.

John almost smiled, then he remembered what Wes had said about Finn crying after the last domestic she dealt with. "You have to toughen up."

"No."

No? "You can't let things like this bother you so much. When you get out of that squad car and it pulls away, you let it take your day with you."

"Fifty years from now, seeing women like Bonnie Lessing and their kids is going to bother me. Watching families get torn apart is going to bother me. I'm not going to let being a cop take that away."

"You won't last five years with that attitude. It'll eat you alive."

Before his very eyes, she changed. The weariness fled from her expression, replaced by something else. Something that looked like trust. And peace. He pushed harder.

"Wes doesn't respect you because of it."

"Because he thinks it makes me soft," Finn agreed. "I think that God wants me to care about people, and I'm not going to let anything squeeze that out of me."

He felt like he'd just hit a brick wall. "So what happens now?"

"I have to meet with Chief Larson and Wes about not following policy," she said simply. "I couldn't wait for backup—it was too dangerous for Bonnie Lessing."

"It was dangerous for you," John said.

"You would have done the same thing. Tell me you wouldn't have."

"That's different," he said, inwardly wincing at the arrogance he heard in his voice.

Finn giggled. She actually giggled. He blinked at the sound.

"I think if you worked here you'd be trying to get rid of me, too."

"Yeah, well I would have succeeded by now," he said.

They were silent for a few minutes. Finn stifled a yawn. "Would you like a cup of tea?"

He winced. "Tea?"

"Too civilized, hmm?" Finn clucked her tongue. "I could try to find something stronger—like battery acid, or drain cleaner."

"You made your point." John grimaced. "Coffee?"

"It'll keep you awake."

"Do you hear me complaining?"

"Coffee it is." Finn stood. "I'm going to change out of my uniform first."

"Into something more comfortable?" His eyes narrowed as she blushed. *Stupid,* he berated himself. *Don't start anything, Gabriel.*

By the time she returned, he already had the coffee going and had found a box of tea bags in her cupboard. "Lemon…orange spice…herbal…who knew they made so many kinds of this stuff?"

"Lemon, please."

He glanced at her and his mouth went dry. He was seriously considering therapy for the first time in his life. Finn's "more comfortable" was a pair of old black sweatpants and a gray T-shirt that had the words "To Protect and To Serve" printed on it, along with an advertisement for a law enforcement charity run. She had taken the pins out of her hair and it swung gently against her shoulders. She was stunning.

"What?" Finn caught him staring.

He tried to summon every ounce of self-control he possessed. He actually felt his face grow warm. "Go sit down and put your feet up," he instructed gruffly. "I'll bring this in."

She gave him such a grateful look that he began searching her cupboards for something sweet to go with the tea. He put their cups on a tray and added a plate of the molasses cookies that she'd doled out to her cousins throughout the weekend.

"My hero. Again." Finn wrapped both hands around the hot cup of tea and closed her eyes blissfully.

"Again?"

"The first time was about ten years ago."

"There was nothing heroic about that," John said after a moment. He took pleasure just in watching her move. Funny how he'd never noticed how graceful a woman could be just drinking a cup of tea. Deliberately, he reined in his wayward thoughts. "That was pure instinct."

"That's why it was heroic. Most people's pure instinct is self-preservation," Finn said. "You saving Chief's life was one of the reasons I decided to become a cop."

"What?" Now she did have his full attention.

"It was. You didn't just save Chief. In a way you saved our whole family. I'm glad God put you there, just at the right time. He knew you'd do the right thing."

"That sounds nice," John said, "but did He have to ruin me in the process?"

"Ruin you?"

He could see that she really didn't know what he was referring to. "My face. My arm." He couldn't quite prevent the sarcasm that leaked out.

"Your face?" She surprised him by laughing. "You've got to be kidding, right? Trust me, there is nothing wrong with your face except that you don't smile enough. And your arm…" She tilted her head and regarded him with an almost whimsical expression on her face. "Let's just say you haven't lost your ability to sweep a girl off her feet, John Gabriel."

The conversation was taking a dangerous path and John suddenly wanted to turn tail and run like a coward. Finn wasn't being flirtatious—she was being honest. Again. He had to do something to break the thread between them.

"I heard you talking to your brother last night when you were by the pool." That did it. She was still, and he could almost see her replaying her conversation with Ryan in her mind. "I think you should take the job."

"You do."

"I think you would be good at it."

"A compliment!" Finn's eyes widened. "Why, John Gabriel, if you keep up this flattery, I'm going to think you care."

He wasn't going to touch that one. "Funny. Are you considering it?"

"Aren't you as good at guessing as you are at eavesdropping?"

"Okay, I deserved that, but I'm not a good guesser where you are concerned."

"I'm praying about it."

He frowned. "So, when are you going to get the telegram? Or is God e-mailing people now?"

"I'm afraid I have to get His response the old-fashioned way," Finn said.

"Right. And that would be…?"

"Through prayer…the Bible…or the counsel of a wise friend."

"I'm your friend." He gave her a wolfish smile.

Finn took a sip of her tea and then stared into the cup. "The fact is, I may not have a choice, which may be an answer right there," she said slowly. "I may be out of a job soon."

"I think Wes might be the one." John finally voiced his suspicions, but even as he spoke the words, there was still that nagging *something* that he couldn't pinpoint. Some instinct that rejected the idea. But who else could it be? The guy was conveniently absent when Finn needed backup at the domestic and then chewed her out for not following department policy. Now he was writing her up and sending her off to the chief.

Finn didn't answer.

"This just may be the war you can't win."

Her eyes lifted from her cup. "Then it's a good thing I don't have to fight the battle alone, isn't it?"

Where did that simple faith come from? There were times when it lit up her eyes like a beacon and made him feel incomplete somehow.

The telephone rang, jarring the silence. He saw the expression of concern on Finn's face and had the same thought—Seamus.

"Hello? Yes, he's right here." She handed him the telephone. "It's for you. It's Neil."

"Gabriel."

"Keeping late hours, aren't we?" Neil's teasing voice came over the line. "Listen, I don't know what your plans are, but pack your bags, buddy, we've got a major breakthrough in the Phelps case. You've got to get back here."

''I'm already packed.'' Adrenaline surged through him. ''I'm on my way.''

John hung up and looked at Finn, who was standing by the door, waiting for him.

''I've got to leave,'' he said unnecessarily. ''California.''

''I'll tell Chief and Anne in the morning.'' Unexpectedly, she moved closer and hugged him.

Briefly, he allowed himself the gift of her embrace. Then he stepped into the darkness.

''Watch your back,'' she whispered.

''You, too.''

Chapter Sixteen

The next morning when Finn went to work, Gil barely glanced at her as she walked in. "They're waiting for you in the chief's office," he said.

Finn realized the grapevine must have already spread the news that she was in trouble. She rapped lightly on Chief Larson's door, opened it and walked in.

"Have a seat, Finn."

Wes was already there, sitting in the other chair.

"Why don't you tell me what happened yesterday at the Lessings'?" Chief Larson said.

Finn began by telling him about the call she'd received from Dispatch and how when she'd arrived at the Lessings' house, she had been waiting for backup but had heard Bonnie Lessing scream. Careful to mention the precautions she'd taken when she entered the house, she told him that Bonnie had been injured and that Jerome had made a threatening move toward his daughter.

"You wrote in your report that you thought Jerome might have been concealing a weapon," Larson said.

Finn suddenly noticed her report was sitting on his desk.

"When Jerome came into the room, he had his hands behind his back," Finn said. "I know that he keeps firearms in the home."

"Which is exactly why we don't want officers playing the Lone Ranger and going into situations like that," Larson said.

"I decided that the threat to Bonnie Lessing was worth the risk to myself—"

"It's not your decision, though," Wes interrupted. "The Police and Fire Commission have made that decision for you in our policy and procedures book. No one goes into a domestic without backup."

Chief Larson glanced at Wes impatiently. "I'm sure Officer Kelly is aware of our policy. But Wes is right. Your presence could have escalated the situation. Jerome doesn't like cops and he has no respect for women. That's two strikes against you. Your actions could have made a dangerous situation even worse."

"And if you'd testified in court against him, the situation wouldn't have come up because he'd be in jail right now," Wes added.

Finn sucked in an angry breath. John had encouraged her to go on the offensive where her job was concerned. "Chief Larson, did Wes mention that he could have provided backup but was taking a phone call at the time?"

"He did mention that." Larson flicked a look at Wes. "The call happened to be from Roger Calhoun, who was calling to complain about your harassment of his son, Ricky."

"What!" Finn couldn't believe it. "Harassment?"

"He said you singled out Ricky for a vandalism complaint when there were several others involved."

"She wanted to arrest him," Wes said, rolling his eyes. "For breaking a few bottles. All he needed was a lesson in good citizenship, so I suggested that he clean up the area."

Larson scratched his head. "Wes, give me a few minutes alone with Finn now. I think you've made your point here."

Wes reluctantly left the room and closed the door behind him.

"Finn, if you had to do this whole thing over with Lessing, what would you do?"

"The same thing."

"I thought so. It's pretty easy to see you've inherited that steel spine from the Kellys." He leaned back in his chair and regarded her seriously. "I've got to make a note of this in your file. And as for the complaint by Roger Calhoun, it does look suspicious that you brought only Ricky in. Wes thought that would cause a problem. Calhoun has a pretty loud voice in this town and he was against you being hired in the first place."

"I understand," Finn said. And she did.

Larson stood up, signaling an end to their conversation. "I guess the next conversation we'll have will be your interview to determine whether you've made your probation."

Finn understood that, too. No more mess-ups.

"Thank you, Chief."

She left his office feeling like a wrung-out dishrag and went to the break room, relieved that no one else was there.

Until Carl walked in.

"Heard you had a pretty rough morning."

"Good news travels fast."

"Don't think that, Finn," Carl said, pulling out a chair and sitting down. "We all get complaints from the good citizens of this town. Dispatch actually had someone dial 911 last week and ask how to make pork chops, then complain the next day to Larson that the dispatcher he got through to wasn't friendly. I mean, come on!"

"I appreciate the pep talk." Finn sighed.

"By the way, it looks like our arsonist is escalating," Carl said.

"Escalating? How?"

"Last night someone saw a suspicious person hanging around the alley and called us. When Parachek got there, the guy was gone but he'd left a gasoline soaked rag on the ground. It was in a neighborhood. Looks like he might have been thinking about torching a house this time."

Finn thought of Ricky Calhoun. "I hope they catch him soon."

"It's just a matter of time. Someone spotted him last night. He's going to make a mistake and then we'll have him."

"So you got pulled through the ringer, huh?" Ryan's voice was full of compassion.

The phone had started ringing just moments after Finn got home from work that afternoon.

"I have just the thing for you," said Ryan.

Finn flopped into her chair and combed her fingers through her hair, propping the telephone between her ear and her shoulder. Briefly she mentally relived the meeting with Chief Larson and Wes. "What's that?"

"On your next day off, come and spend some time with your big brother."

"Sounds good. Is there chocolate ice cream involved?"

Ryan laughed. "Would you come if there wasn't?"

Finn pretended to consider it. "I might."

"Any word from John Gabriel?"

She dodged the question. "Should there be?"

"He left his cell phone number with me."

"He what?" Finn sat up in surprise.

"He called me from somewhere and gave me his cell phone number. He was worried about Chief and wanted us to track him down if we needed to."

"Oh." Finn was touched by his concern.

"The way he talked, it sounded like it would be a few weeks before he came back to town."

"I'm off next Monday," Finn said, glancing at her calendar.

"I have an ulterior motive, you know."

"I figured you did."

"I want you to help me interview some of my volunteers," Ryan confessed. "I could use your input."

"I'd love to help out," Finn said, meaning it. Anything to keep her mind off her trouble at the department. She hung up the phone and felt an emptiness she couldn't shake off. It had followed her like a shadow.

Finn tried not to dwell on the fact that John would be gone for an indefinite amount of time. And then what? He was officially out of her life now. He had done his duty. Fulfilled his promise to Chief. She didn't know why she felt such a loss. He was exasperating. Bitter. Sometimes downright unkind. Unless he was ordering her to put her feet up and serving her tea and cookies…

''Man looks at the outward, but God looks at the heart.''

The verse about David came to mind, only this time she thought about it in reference to John.

Finn wasn't even convinced John Gabriel had a heart anymore. *Lord, I know You're good at surprises. I know You want John to belong to You. You know the best way to reach him. I'm trusting You on this one.*

Ryan was sitting at his desk looking slightly harassed when she walked into his office at The Wild Olive on Monday. Sweat beaded his forehead and Finn pulled at the collar of her shirt.

''It's like a furnace in here.''

''Tell me about it!'' Ryan groaned. ''The air conditioner has been broken for three days. I feel like a rotisserie chicken.''

Finn laughed. ''What can I do?''

''Don't you want lunch first?''

''You're just being polite,'' Finn said. ''We can take some time off later. I'll feel better if you can go out for lunch without thinking about everything you left undone.''

''You are a princess, Finn.'' Ryan looked relieved. ''I have some applications from people interested in volunteering. One of them called—I'm not sure which one because Sharon writes my messages down in invisible ink—and she's supposed to be coming in this morning. Maybe you could look through these and do some weeding right away to save us some time. Like this one. Look at her address!''

Finn bent over and saw the name of one of the most prominent neighborhoods in Chicago.

''No doubt some society girl who wants to add a

charity to her list of achievements. She'll come in once and then start sending a check instead—'' Ryan's voice broke off suddenly, and Finn followed his gaze to the door.

A young woman was standing there. She was tall and willowy, with a tousled cap of short dark hair and the angular features of a model. Despite the heat, she looked stunningly fresh in a white linen sundress.

''Can I help you?'' Ryan asked politely.

She flashed him a friendly smile. ''Are you Ryan Kelly?''

Ryan stood. ''Yes, I am.''

''I'm Celia Greyson-Fletcher, the society girl.''

Ryan gulped audibly. ''I—''

''May I use your phone please?''

''Of course.'' Ryan motioned to the desk.

She stepped around him, nodding briefly at Finn as she picked up the telephone and punched in some numbers.

''Good morning, Mr. Gibson. This is Celia. I would like you to call someone about installing a new air-conditioning system at The Wild Olive Family Shelter. Today if possible. Right. Thank you very much.'' She hung up the telephone and looked at Ryan. ''I am here for my interview.''

Ryan looked at Finn, his eyes full of panic. She took pity on him immediately. ''I'm helping my brother with interviews today,'' she said. ''I'm Fiona Kelly, but call me Finn.''

''It's nice to meet you.'' Celia smiled and fanned herself with her white straw hat. ''It is warm, isn't it. Where would you like me to sit?''

''Here, take my chair. I've got some other things to do—'' Ryan said in a rush.

Finn couldn't remember ever seeing her brother so flustered.

"I'll be back later, Finn. Miss Greyson-Fletcher," he added.

"Please, call me Celia."

With another strangled sound, Ryan bolted from the room.

Finn grinned. "You handled that well, Celia."

Celia grinned impishly. "Thank you. I'm sorry to see he has such a low opinion of the Gold Coast."

"I think the heat is affecting him, he's not usually so cranky," Finn offered honestly. She grabbed a pen and fished through the drawers for some paper. "Let's start with the basics. Why did you apply for a volunteer position with The Wild Olive?"

"Each Sunday the pastor of our church brings up the name of a shelter or soup kitchen for prayer," Celia said. "Two weeks ago, it was The Wild Olive. I was intrigued because it sounded like so much more that a typical shelter."

"It is," Finn agreed. "There are small apartments upstairs, most designed for families. That was Ryan's idea. The Wild Olive takes in women and children who are trying to relocate from some of the housing projects and start over. The Wild Olive works with churches to sponsor a family and locate housing, employment, even child care if necessary, and then they follow up for a year. Usually by that time, the shelter has worked itself out of a job."

"The whole idea intrigued me," Celia said.

"Do you have any experience working in a setting like this?"

Celia laughed. "None."

Finn tried again. "What do you think your gifts and abilities are?"

"I've studied cooking in France for the past six months." Celia smiled winsomely. "Do you need a chef?"

Finn found herself smiling back. There was something very appealing about Celia Greyson-Fletcher. "They do need cooks occasionally."

"There you go, then. I make a terrific beef burgundy and very light pastries."

"I'll tell you what positions are open and you tell me where you can help." Finn settled back in the rickety chair. "They need counselors, housekeepers and someone to facilitate a parenting group…"

Celia was listening intently as Finn read through the list, but her expression didn't change. Finn felt a stab of regret, reluctant to suggest that maybe Celia would be better suited somewhere else. Then, an idea struck her. "My brother has been offered the position of director," she said suddenly. "Which would leave his current position open."

Celia's eyes sparkled with interest. "What does he do now?"

"A little bit of everything."

That slow smile curved Celia's mouth. "Finn, I can do that!"

As they sat smiling at each other, Ryan ventured back into the room.

"What's going on?" he asked Finn suspiciously.

"Celia is interested in your position."

Ryan gaped at her. "My position!"

"If you take over as director, I mean." Finn crossed her arms in satisfaction.

"It isn't a volunteer position," Ryan protested. "It's

a paid position and very demanding. It isn't something you can fit in between tennis and brunch.''

"Ryan!" Finn was taken aback by Ryan's heartless words. He was always willing to give someone a chance to prove themselves.

Celia sat up a little bit straighter, if that were possible, and lifted her chin. "Perhaps you would accept my application for review and we can go from there, Pastor Kelly."

Ryan looked like he was choking. "Fine."

"My brother and I were just going to have lunch," Finn said. "Would you like to join us, Celia?"

She ignored Ryan's muffled gasp. "I'd love to."

Finn knew she would be in trouble when she and Ryan were alone, but fortunately that wouldn't be for a while. Celia didn't blink at the choice of the tiny corner café that Ryan took them to down the street. To her credit, she brushed the crumbs off the vinyl seat without a word and smiled warmly at the waitress.

"Do you live in Chicago, Finn?" Celia asked, sipping her ice water delicately.

"I live in Miranda Station, Wisconsin. It's about three hours from here."

"I've never heard of it," Celia said reflectively. "I thought maybe you worked at The Wild Olive."

"I wanted her to take over my position," Ryan said grimly.

"I have a job, thank you."

"And that is…" Celia looked at her expectantly.

"I'm a police officer."

The serene expression on Celia's face dissolved. "You aren't!"

Ryan grinned at her reaction.

"I really am," Finn said.

"They make her carry a pretend gun, though—" Ryan winced as Finn buried her elbow into his side. "Ouch!"

"I didn't mean to offend you," Celia said sincerely. "It's just that you—"

"Don't look like a cop," Finn sighed. "I know. You're not the first to say so."

"Tell us a little about yourself, Celia," Ryan said suddenly.

Celia's green-eyed gaze swung to him and she said evenly, "You seem to know all about me."

"Touché," Ryan muttered. "Fill in some of the blanks for me, would you?"

Finn watched her brother with amusement. Ryan glanced at Celia, then looked away and fiddled with his napkin.

"I have a degree in Art Therapy," she said, surprising even Finn with that bit of information. "And six months' experience in French cooking. I do play tennis quite well, but I never go out for brunch."

Ryan colored slightly.

"Art Therapy?"

"I know it sounds a little unconventional." Celia shrugged. "I just graduated last spring and I've been traveling quite a bit for the past year."

Finn and Ryan glanced at each other. *Jet-setting,* Ryan's expression said plainly. Finn flashed him a warning look.

"Contrary to what you may think, Pastor Kelly, I am looking for employment. I don't get bored easily and I am able to work under pressure."

"Why don't you come back tomorrow and we can talk about the specifics of the job," Ryan said briskly.

Finn could tell what he was thinking about Celia.

That she'd jump into her Mercedes and leave skid marks on the pavement when she found out more about his job.

"That would be fine."

"And thank you for the new air-conditioning system," Ryan added reluctantly.

"Pastor Kelly, I've discovered that money has a purpose…it is very helpful to further God's kingdom in practical ways," Celia said candidly. "He gave me an opportunity to dispense it as He leads and I'm thankful for that."

Finn tried to hide her smile. Her brother looked totally bemused. It wasn't often that she saw him off balance. She said a quick, silent prayer of thanks for Celia Greyson-Fletcher's unexpected entrance into Ryan's life.

As they walked back to The Wild Olive, Finn glanced at her watch. "I would like to call Diane Avery and find out how the baby is doing."

Celia made arrangements to come back the following day, and then Ryan trailed behind Finn to his office.

"She's something, isn't she?" Finn said, unable to resist teasing her brother.

"Who's something? Oh, you mean Celia Greyson-Fletcher." He accentuated every syllable of her name in a snooty, fake British accent.

Finn elbowed him playfully in the side. "Looks like you may have a new assistant."

He scowled at her. "I wanted *you* to be my assistant. Remember?"

"I think Celia will do a spectacular job."

"Oh sure. An art therapist who can make fancy pastries."

"Admit it—you liked her."

Ryan actually flushed. "She was wearing a ring, didn't you notice?"

"No." Finn was surprised.

"It looked like an engagement ring."

Finn caught her bottom lip between her teeth. "Really?"

"She won't show tomorrow," Ryan predicted. "She'll wake up tomorrow morning and decide to go shopping in Paris instead."

Finn reached the desk and put her finger to her lips as she dialed. "No, she won't... Hello? Is this Diane?" Now that she had Diane on the telephone, Finn felt suddenly nervous. After all, she'd only met Diane once and the visit was brief at that. "This is Finn Kelly. Do you remember—"

Diane's excited squeal on the other end told her that she did. "Finn Kelly! Are you in Chicago?"

"I'm visiting my brother, Ryan, for a few days this week," Finn explained. "I just thought I'd call to say hello."

"Neil is out of town, so it's just Deborah and me," Diane said. "Can I convince you to come over and visit for a while? I've been alone almost a week now and I'm going crazy for some adult conversation."

Finn jotted down her address and pushed it over to Ryan.

"You can be there in half an hour," he whispered.

"I'll be there as soon as I can," Finn promised.

"Great."

Diane sounded so relieved that Finn laughed before saying goodbye and hanging up.

"She sounds like she could use some company," Ryan commented.

"You don't mind, do you?"

"Not a bit. I've got to get some paperwork in order just in case Miss Celia Greyson-Fletcher does show up tomorrow morning," Ryan said.

"She'll be here." Finn grabbed her purse, kissed her brother on the cheek and hurried out the door.

To her surprise, the Averys lived within a mile of John's apartment complex. It was a newer two-story colonial-style farmhouse but fit its country setting as if it had been built a hundred years before. Flowers bordered the sidewalk and pots of geraniums swung gently from wrought-iron hangers on the old-fashioned porch.

Even before she reached the front door, Diane was hurrying out to meet her.

"I've got the coffee already poured," she said. "Deborah is taking her afternoon nap, so that will give us some time to catch up."

Finn followed her into the kitchen and was charmed by the informal, breezy decor. "You have a lovely home."

"Thank you." Diane smiled. "I understand you do, too."

Finn frowned slightly and Diane noticed. "John told us."

She blinked. "John told you?" she repeated cautiously.

"He told us you said his decorator should be in jail, too," Diane laughed.

Finn felt the color flood into her face. "I didn't mean—"

"Oh, don't worry, he wasn't offended," Diane interrupted, handing her a delicate china cup filled with steaming coffee. "He knows it's the truth. I've been trying to get him to do something to that place for a long time. Let's sit outside, shall we? It's such a gorgeous day and I've brought the baby monitor.''

Finn settled into one of the wicker chairs on the porch.

"They're together, you know," Diane said. "Neil and John. They've been working on this investigation for over a year now, following different leads. Months will go by without anything, and then the next thing I know, they're on a plane to who-knows-where."

Finn realized she was starved for news about John. "Do you have any idea when they're coming home?"

Diane shook her head. "Neil calls whenever he gets a chance. He misses Deborah terribly, but it's the nature of the job. I've been watering John's plant." She winked at Finn.

"I'm surprised he still has it," Finn murmured, remembering the way he grumbled about taking care of it.

Diane's eyes widened. "Are you kidding? He told me to make sure I spritz it with warm water and rotate it once a week to—and I quote—'give it the maximum benefit of the sun.'"

Finn laughed. "Really?"

"He was very specific in his instructions," Diane said. "In fact, I have to run over there today when Deborah wakes up. Care to ride along?"

"Sure."

They talked for over an hour until Deborah woke up. Finn watched with a mixture of awe and envy as Diane cuddled the baby and cooed to her. Deborah's skin was like porcelain and her dark hair lay in soft curls on her head.

After Deborah was fed, Diane buckled her into the infant car seat and they headed to John's apartment.

"It's such a pretty apartment complex," Finn ventured.

"Thank you." Diane winked at Finn and adjusted the rearview mirror. "It's not like he had much of a choice, though. He lived in this tiny apartment downtown when we met him. If you can believe it, that place was actually *worse* than this one, as far as his lack of furnishings. When there was an opening here he was out of town, so I went ahead and put the deposit down on it. When he got back, I told him he was moving."

Finn couldn't imagine anyone being so pushy with John Gabriel. But it obviously worked!

"He's used to me," Diane said, as if reading her thoughts. "I remember when Neil introduced us for the first time...he had this invisible 'do not disturb' sign on him but I just felt God telling us to reach out to him."

"He isn't the easiest man to know," Finn acknowledged quietly.

Diane glanced at her. "You've been good for him."

"What?"

"You've been good for him," Diane repeated matter-of-factly. "Both Neil and I have noticed a change in him since he met you."

"I don't think it's because of me," Finn said, shaken by the other woman's observation.

"We'll see," Diane said cryptically. "Well, here we are." She turned the car into John's parking space and shut off the engine. "Home sweet home."

Diane unlocked the apartment while Finn held Deborah. Then they walked inside and Finn was once again depressed by its sparse interior. The tree was lush and healthy looking, though, and she smiled when she saw it.

"Sad, isn't it?" Diane said with a sigh, referring to the apartment.

"Yes, it is," Finn agreed. She gave Deborah back to her mother and wandered through the rest of the apartment. Peeking into his bedroom, she saw a tumble of clothes on the bed as if he had been in a hurry to leave. Without thinking, she walked in and started to fold them.

"Do you think your brother would mind if you spent the night with us? We could have dinner together," Diane called out.

"I could do that," Finn said, coming out of the bedroom. "Ryan is always swamped with work, and I could run over and help him again in the morning." She enjoyed Diane Avery's company, and she knew Diane was someone whose friendship she could value. Between her job and keeping a watchful eye on her grandparents, Finn hadn't had much opportunity to make friends in Miranda Station. She realized now how much she missed having another woman to talk to.

"That would be great," Diane said cheerfully. "You'll just have to tell me if I talk your ear off!"

The telephone ringing surprised both of them and Deborah started to cry. Finn hurried over to the phone. "I'll get it."

"Hello?"

There was a moment of silence. "Diane."

"No..." Finn recognized John's voice immediately and she suddenly lost her breath.

"Finn?" He sounded like he couldn't believe it was her.

"Ah, y-yes, it's me," Finn stammered. "I'm here with Diane. We're watering your plant."

"I tried their house and there was no answer, so I thought she might be at my place," John said.

"I was just visiting," Finn said. "Ryan and I had lunch together and I called Diane afterward. We ended up getting together at their house this afternoon."

"I'm flying back tomorrow," John told her. "Will you still be there?"

"I'm staying until Wednesday." Finn glanced at Diane, who was spritzing his plant while Deborah cooed at the drapes.

"How is Chief doing?"

"He's doing great." Finn couldn't disguise the relief in her voice.

"And your meeting with the powers-that-be?"

"All right. I guess I'll know for sure in a few weeks, won't I."

There was a moment of silence. John glanced around the interior of the motel room. A huge cockroach scuttled into a crack in the wall. Just hearing Finn's voice made him feel better. Cleaner.

"How is my plant?" He closed his eyes and could almost see Finn's smile.

"Thriving."

"What have you done this time?" John asked suddenly, his voice thick with suspicion.

"Done?"

"You know, the last time it was a high-maintenance plant, a pizza and a cupboard full of groceries," he reminded her.

"Oh, we just got here," Finn said innocently. "We haven't had time to sabotage anything. Yet."

"Put Diane on."

Finn felt curiously disappointed at his sudden, curt tone. "He wants to talk to you, Diane."

Diane grinned and took the phone. "Where is my husband? What? Are you kidding?" A slow smile spread across her face. "It wouldn't be any trouble at all! We've got all evening. My sister has been begging for a chance to watch Deborah." A wink in Finn's direction. "Did you have anything in particular in mind? Great, and tell Neil that I love him."

Diane hung up the telephone and her expression was a mixture of wonder and disbelief.

"What happened?" Finn asked.

"We're going shopping," Diane said.

"Shopping?"

"You aren't going to believe this, Finn. John told me to go ahead and overhaul his apartment. He said we were most likely plotting to do it anyway. He actually told me to go out and buy some things for it."

"Like furniture?" Finn said hopefully.

"He said—and I quote—'Whatever you think would look good.' Unquote. Are you up to it?"

Finn grinned. "Are you?"

Diane laughed. "Are you kidding? Let's go."

The next morning, Finn let herself into John's apartment for some finishing touches. She couldn't believe the transformation herself when she came inside. A nervous flutter rose in her stomach. What if he hated it? She and Deborah had tackled the project with efficiency and speed. It was almost comical the way they gravitated toward the same colors and accessories. At one point, they were an aisle apart and both of them rushed toward the other holding the same vase! Their laughter had rippled through the store, causing several weary clerks to smile.

At eight o'clock, most of the furniture would be delivered. Finn glanced at her watch. She was planning to go back to The Wild Olive a little later. She had called Ryan from Diane's and found out he'd had an emergency with one of the families he saw on a regular basis and had to leave the shelter. She made a pot of coffee and waited for the deliverymen to arrive.

By ten, the new furniture was in place. Finn was already tired. The deliverymen had been helpful but were on a tight schedule. She ended up doing some relocating of the furniture after they'd gone. The beige couch had disappeared, stuffed into the truck and taken away. Finn moved past the soft russet-and-cream checked sofa, running her fingers across the birch trim on the back. The matching chairs faced the landscaped gardens out the window. An enormous basket of dried eucalyptus and flowers graced the new coffee table.

In the dining room, there was now an oval oak table with matching chairs. It was small but expandable with the leaves hidden inside. She and Diane had had some time to pick out a few pieces of artwork for the walls and were satisfied with what they'd chosen. Minutes before the store closed, Diane actually let out a whoop of excitement when Finn showed her the bedroom set she'd found, tucked in the back of the antique store.

"It's perfect!" she'd exclaimed. "He'll love it."

"M-maybe he should pick out his own bedroom set," Finn stammered. "I mean, a bedroom set is pretty personal, isn't it?"

"He said get whatever looked nice," Diane reminded her gleefully.

Finn was almost sorry she wouldn't be there to see John's face when he walked in....

She fished her car keys out of her purse, opened the door—and came face-to-face with John.

"John." She blinked in surprise.

He shook his head in bemusement, as if eyes were playing tricks on him. "Took my offer seriously, did you?" He moved past her and stopped dead in his tracks. The suitcase he was holding fell to the floor with a dull *thud*. Slowly, his eyes swept over the changes.

Finn tried desperately to imagine them through his eyes. She and Diane had managed to use a blend of neutral colors and clean lines while avoiding large, chunky pieces of furniture and the traditional masculine colors of black and brown. Instead, they had accented with ivory and hunter green.

Stunned, John wandered into the kitchen and almost bumped into the table and chairs that hadn't been there before.

"I hope we didn't spend too much of your money," Finn said. She couldn't tell by the expression on his face whether he liked it or not.

"I talked to you at what time yesterday...three?" He turned on her and barked out the question.

"I think it was around three," Finn murmured.

"And you managed to do all this." His sweeping gesture encompassed the two rooms.

"Actually," Finn confessed, "we did more than this."

"More?"

"We found..."

But John was already heading down the hall to his bedroom. Finn quickly followed. The bedroom set she had chosen was a little unique. She wasn't sure what he was going to think.

He stood for a moment looking into the room. "What is this called?" he asked quietly.

Finn bit her lip. It was hard not to laugh, and he must have heard something in her voice because he speared her with a quick glance. "It's a sleigh bed."

"A sleigh bed," he repeated.

"You hate it," Finn said dismally. "I picked it out. I'm sorry. I know it's not everyone's taste but I couldn't resist. They're beautiful, I think, but you're a man and you probably want something square and—"

"I like it."

The simple words cut through her rambling and Finn stared at him. "You do?"

He prowled around the bed and examined the new dresser that matched it. There were flowers on his nightstand. Fresh flowers. And a large round candle.

"You and Diane are miracle workers. I think you missed your calling." He actually smiled. "Now I suppose I have to sell my car to pay for all of this."

Finn wasn't sure whether he was serious or not, then she saw the light in his eyes. He was actually teasing her! "And your old baseball card collection," she said.

His eyebrow lifted. "Baseball card collection?"

"Don't all little boys collect baseball cards?" she asked, remembering Ryan's shoe boxes full.

An odd look passed over his face, extinguishing the light that had been there momentarily. "Probably most boys."

Finn realized her mistake at once. *From foster home to foster home,* her grandmother had said. There probably had been no collection for him at all. "It's never too late," she said seriously.

He had missed her. The thought struck him with the intensity of a shock wave. In the past, he had come home from investigations to the empty apartment feeling almost sorry that he was back. This time, he admitted to himself, he had been looking forward to seeing what Finn and Diane had done to his apartment. He had expected minor changes—maybe another plant or new towels in the bathroom. But when the door had opened and he saw Finn standing there, he knew that what he'd really wanted to see was her. *She* was in Chicago. That was what had had him taking the red-eye flight from California.

As he stood in silence, Finn could see the lines of fatigue around his eyes. "Let me pour you a cup of coffee."

"I don't think I have any."

"You do now." Finn smiled at him.

They walked into the kitchen and he sat down at the table. "A real table."

"And real chairs." She easily located one of the two coffee cups he had and sat down opposite him. "How did it go?"

"We've wrapped it up," John told her.

"Can you tell me about it?"

So he did. At one point, she slipped out of the chair and poured them both another cup of coffee as she listened to his story, following the twists and turns of a long investigation that had finally come to end.

"How about lunch?" John said unexpectedly.

"You want me to make you lunch?"

"No, I want to take you out for lunch." John smiled the smile that always managed to give her heart a double kick. "To thank you for what you did to my apartment."

She wanted to spend more time with him. And she wanted to run as far as she could in the other direction.

John watched the play of emotions on her face. He could identify them because he was feeling exactly the same way. He hadn't meant to offer to take her out. But he wasn't ready for her to leave, either. It seemed right that she was there somehow. How she asked him to share details of the investigation, listening closely and occasionally asking questions. He had already been debriefed at the agency for two hours, but it was different telling Finn about it. She was more concerned with how he *felt* than what he had done.

"Where are we going? Do I look all right?" Finn wondered aloud, her way of accepting his invitation.

John's eyes swept over her. She was wearing blue jeans and a denim shirt with a scattering of flowers embroidered on the collar. Her hair was pulled back into some sort of braid that drew immediate attention to her unusual eyes and beautiful face.

"We won't go anywhere fancy."

She looked relieved. "Great."

The place he chose was a half-hour drive away and it served seafood. After the meal, they lingered for an hour over cheesecake and coffee, and John was amazed how relaxed he felt. Until they walked out into the parking lot.

Two young men were smoking cigarettes by the car and they both stopped talking abruptly as Finn and John walked toward them. One leaned forward and peered at Finn and the simple movement sent his body off balance. He had been drinking—probably all night and straight through breakfast and lunch.

"Hey, sweetheart." He grinned widely and nudged his companion.

"Here chicky, chicky, chicky," the other called, then collapsed against the hood of his car, laughing.

"I like redheads," the first one leered.

John moved ahead of Finn slightly, and the leering one stepped back.

"Excuse us," he said with icy politeness.

"Oh, you poor girl!" He shook his head at Finn in mock sympathy as he noticed John's empty sleeve. "Don't stay with him 'cause you feel sorry for him. Let me show you what a real man can do."

"It's you I feel sorry for," Finn said before John could react. "And as a police officer, I would suggest that you call someone to drive you home…" John saw her read the plate number on the car. "Or I could call the local precinct and they'll make sure you have a designated driver."

"She ain't no cop," the other sneered. "She's bluffing you."

"Actually, we both are in law enforcement," Finn said. "Isn't that right, Agent Gabriel?"

John could see they found that less believable than Finn being an officer. He had dealt with this over the years but for some reason it seared him now like an open wound. He wasn't sure what the outcome of this unexpected confrontation was going to be, but he wasn't going to let Finn get verbally mauled by these two.

"A skinny chick and a one-armed man," the other laughed. "Give me a break!"

Finn had obviously had enough. She pulled out her badge and flashed it in front of their astonished faces.

"You make that call or I'll make one from my cell phone."

"Right, uh, officer," one of them gulped, and they both headed back toward the bar they'd stumbled from.

They got into John's car and rode in silence for several minutes. When John glanced at Finn, he saw the outline of her profile as she stared out the window. He wondered what she was thinking. That he was inadequate as a protector? That she had to protect *him?*

"Finn." He may have been experienced in interrogations but he was finding out he was lousy at trying to see into the mind of this particular young woman. "What's wrong?"

"I hate it when people call me skinny." The words came out in an emotional rush.

There was absolute silence in the car for a moment…and then John burst out laughing.

Chapter Seventeen

With a few clicks of the mouse, a series of photos dotted the screen of the computer. His stomach clenched at the grainy images and he looked up at Neil, who was standing beside him.

"I'd say we've got everything we need right here."

Neil's face was pale. "Let's call it in."

A door slammed downstairs and both men froze.

"Who do you suppose that is?" Neil muttered, his hand automatically moving under his jacket to the 9mm tucked in the holster under his jacket.

"If I had to guess, I'd say trouble," John said grimly.

Finn was sitting at the kitchen table paying bills when someone rapped on the front door.

"Ryan! What brings you here?" She threw herself into his arms.

"My favorite sister," he said with a lopsided smile.

"Come in!" She linked her arm with his and started to pull him inside, but he resisted.

"I brought someone with me."

Finn looked over his shoulder and saw Celia Greyson-Fletcher standing just outside.

"Celia!" Finn said in surprise. "I didn't see you there. Come in."

Having Ryan unexpectedly appear at her door was one thing, but seeing him accompanied by Celia Greyson-Fletcher had Finn trying to hide a smile. Maybe she had inherited some of her grandfather's matchmaking tendencies after all!

With an almost hesitant smile, Celia started forward. "Hello, Finn."

"Have you two been over to see Chief and Gran yet?" Finn asked.

"Not yet," Ryan said. He and Celia followed her inside and Finn went right into the kitchen. "Let me get you something to drink. Coffee or tea?"

"Tea."

"Coffee."

They responded simultaneously, and Finn laughed. "All right, you two, make it difficult for me. Now really, what's going on?"

"Diane Avery called me yesterday."

"Diane!" Finn looked at him in surprise. "Why?"

Ryan hesitated, and Finn's heart took a sudden dive. *"What?"*

"She asked me to pray for Neil. And for John."

"Ryan…"

"They're missing," Ryan said quietly. "They've been out of contact for three days now. Both of them. She asked me to let you know. She tried to call you yesterday but she didn't get an answer and she was going to fly out to Washington D.C. early this morning. That's where they were. Following some guy who was a former FBI agent or something."

Finn couldn't believe it. Diane had told her that Neil called daily, no matter what.

"I'm sorry, Finn," Celia said softly. "I know they're close friends of yours."

Close friends. The words mocked Finn. John wasn't close to anyone. Just when she thought his walls were beginning to crumble, self-preservation put them firmly in place. For a week since her return to Miranda Station, she had struggled with her feelings for him. She hoped he would call and yet was afraid to answer the phone in case he did. Finally, she took all her longings and fears, carried them to the Lord and left them there. Now this...

"I didn't want to tell you over the phone," Ryan explained quietly. "Can we pray with you about this?"

Finn nodded. "Please."

Half an hour passed as they lifted not only the two men up in prayer but also Diane and Deborah.

"I'll leave you two alone for a few minutes. I'm going over to tell Seamus and Gran," Ryan said. "I wanted you to know first, Finn."

After he'd gone, Finn refilled Celia's teacup. "It was nice of you to come with Ryan."

"Nice had nothing to do with it," Celia said. "I simply told him I was coming with him and he didn't have a choice."

Finn chuckled. Ryan had told her that he had given Celia the job but he had sounded rather dazed by the fact, as if he still couldn't figure out how it had happened. "How do you like working there?"

"I love it," Celia said honestly. "Your brother is very committed and he has more energy than a two-year-old."

Finn laughed at the comparison. "Don't you have any brothers or sisters?"

"I'm an only child. Actually, my parents adopted me when I was two. Some of the relatives didn't want 'outside blood' mingling with the Greyson-Fletcher line, but my parents said they fell in love with me the second they saw me. Most people want infants, you know, but that didn't matter to them." Celia smiled with obvious affection. "They're very stubborn!"

Something clicked in Finn's memory.

My sister and I were split into different foster homes when she was two and I was nine.

What was her name?

Celia.

"Finn!" Celia's voice seemed to come from a long distance away. "Finn! What's wrong?"

Finn blinked and realized that Celia had her arm around her. Their faces were inches apart. And she was staring into two deep green eyes. Celia's eyes. Eyes that were just like John's.

"It can't be," Finn whispered.

"Let's go outside for some fresh air," Celia said worriedly. "This has been too much for you."

"No." Finn shook her head. "I think…" Could she even verbalize it? What if she was wrong? "I think that you and John Gabriel may be related."

Celia frowned, obviously worried that the troubling news they had brought Finn had affected her somehow. "Finn, I just told you I was adopted," she said patiently as she glanced out the window, clearly hoping that Ryan was on his way back.

"John told me once that he and his sister were separated when she was two and he was nine," Finn said. "And that her name was Celia."

Celia stared at her. "That's impossible. I didn't have a sibling. My mother told me once that if I'd had any brothers or sisters, they would have adopted them, too."

"Maybe they didn't know."

"Finn, it has to be a coincidence." Tears filled Celia's eyes. "It can't be."

Finn drew a slow breath and realized that it hurt. "I don't know."

"Was he in Chicago at the time?" Celia asked. "Do you know who his mother was?"

"He doesn't share much about his life," Finn said. "He just said he tried to find you when he was older but he couldn't because you'd been privately adopted. He was in foster care all those years."

The weight of the last statement wasn't lost on either of them. *Oh, God, I don't understand. If he is Celia's brother, why couldn't he have lived with the Greyson-Fletchers and grown up in a family who loved him...and who loved You? Why?*

"We have to find out for sure," Celia said. Her voice was steady but emotion churned in her eyes. "I'll talk to my parents when Ryan and I drive back this evening."

They sat in silence for a few minutes, each lost in thought. Finally Celia said, "Tell me about him."

"He's thirty-three. Did Ryan tell you that he saved Seamus after an explosion in a warehouse ten years ago?"

"He told me on the way here."

"He lost part of his arm, but I think he's lost a whole lot more than that, Celia. He's got so many barriers up. Just about the time I feel him softening, it's like he reminds himself that he isn't allowed to be happy. He

questions my faith and yet I sense a longing there.''
Finn shook her head. ''Diane and Neil Avery are the
only people he's let into his life.''

''It sounds to me like he's let you in, too,'' Celia
murmured.

Finn's eyes widened. ''I don't think so.''

''From what Ryan has told me, it sounds like he's
been spending a lot of time with you.''

''That's because Chief asked him to,'' Finn said
darkly.

''I hope that if he is my brother he'll let me be part
of his life, too,'' Celia said. ''I can't imagine the life
he's lived so far. It could have been so different.''

Ryan returned then and threw himself into the chair
opposite Finn, momentarily unaware of the emotional
currents in the room. ''Chief is already on the phone
to the Madison Agency to find out everything he can.''

Finn and Celia exchanged looks. At Celia's nod,
Finn put her hand on her brother's. ''We have something to tell you.''

At midnight, the telephone rang. Finn, who had been
praying for over an hour, grabbed it. ''Hello?''

''It's Celia.''

Finn had known it would be. She had told Celia to
call, no matter what time it was.

''Did you find out anything?''

''My dad made some phone calls this evening. I
haven't seen him this upset in a long time. He finally
talked to a former social worker who had been a co-
worker of the woman who handled our file.''

Our file.

''I did…I *do* have a brother, Finn. The social worker
lied to my parents, plain and simple. She figured they

wouldn't be interested in a nine-year-old boy as part of the package, so she conveniently didn't mention him. She sent us to two different foster homes, and two weeks later, when they came to see me, I was an 'only child.'"

"So the social worker thinks that John might be your brother?"

"I know John is my brother," Celia said. "Everything matches up. Our mother voluntarily terminated her rights to us when I was eighteen months old, but my last name was Gabriel."

Blinded by tears, Finn reached for the box of tissue as she listened.

"And the worst part of it is, I may never get to meet him—" Celia's voice broke off raggedly. "I've been praying and so have Mom and Dad. Dad has been pacing the floor most of the evening. To think all these years we've been living in the same city…"

Finn tried to comfort Celia, but it was difficult because she needed some comforting herself. With a promise to talk again the next day, Finn hung up the phone.

And it rang again. She thought maybe Celia had forgotten to tell her something and then she heard Diane's voice.

"Finn?"

"Diane." She sank back into the cushions of the chair and closed her eyes. For the first time since she'd met Diane, the other woman's voice sounded weary. Stripped of emotion. Finn was afraid of what she was going to hear.

"I'm calling to tell you that I'm still in a hotel in D.C. but we'll be flying back into Chicago tomorrow."

"Did you say 'we'll'?" Finn grabbed onto the word hopefully.

"I can't talk now, but I needed to tell you so you wouldn't worry. They're both safe and sound, praise the Lord," Diane said, her voice cracking slightly.

"And John? He's all right, too?"

There was a moment's hesitation. "He's fine."

Finn heard someone say something to her in the background.

"Finn, if you're thinking about meeting the plane, I think you should reconsider. They're both pretty exhausted."

Something in her voice didn't sound quite right but Finn was still overwhelmed by the fact that John and Neil were safe. Thank You, God.

"Diane, thank you for calling."

"I'll let you know when we get home," Diane said with forced cheerfulness. Then her voice lowered to a whisper. "Keep praying, Finn."

Less than a week later, Finn stood beside her brother's desk at The Wild Olive and glanced at the clock for the fiftieth time. Ryan pretended to catch up on some paperwork and Celia stood by the window, waiting for the first glimpse of her brother. "He'll be here soon."

Celia nodded calmly but Finn wasn't fooled. The truth was, all three of them were nervous about this reunion. Diane had called Finn when she, Neil and John had returned to Chicago, but she hadn't been able to give Finn specifics over the phone. All she could say was that the men had had a "harrowing" experience in D.C. and now John seemed more distant than usual. Neil was concerned about him, too.

Knowing how anxious Celia was to meet John, Finn finally called him. To her dismay, his emotional barriers were firmly in place once again. Considering he'd been the one to initiate their last lunch together, it seemed odd that he was now guarded and had only reluctantly accepted her invitation to meet. She hadn't said anything about Celia. As a police officer, she knew there was some news that couldn't be given over the telephone.

"He's here." Celia turned away from the window and a few moments later, John appeared in the doorway.

"Hi." Finn's voice sounded strained even to her own ears. She was relieved to see him, she had to fight the temptation to run straight into his embrace. Instead, she squeezed Celia's hand.

John felt suddenly vulnerable—as if he were about to be ambushed. Before he could speak, however, Finn and Ryan slipped out of the office and left him alone with the young woman who stood beside the desk, regarding him solemnly. There were tears in her eyes. He wondered briefly if she were in some kind of trouble and that's why Finn had contacted him.

"Is there something I can do for you?" he asked, disturbed by the shattered expression on her face.

"I...my name is Celia Greyson-Fletcher," she said quietly. "I'm your sister."

Celia. John tried to reconcile the beautiful woman standing in front of him with the chubby, wispy-haired toddler he remembered.

"I know this is a shock," Celia was saying, "and I understand if you need some time to think about it, but my...parents...would like to meet you, too."

A shock. That was an understatement. He thought that hiding for three days in the basement of a crack house armed with evidence against a crooked FBI agent— who just happened to have ''people'' looking for them—had thrown off his equilibrium. Now, he felt as if he were being sucked into a bottomless hole. *His sister.* For a moment, pride welled up inside of him. How many nights had he been tortured with the thought that she was unhappy or neglected? Now, after all these years, he could put his worst fears to rest. It was obvious that the poised woman standing several feet away had been well taken care of. Pampered and loved. It was what he had always wished for her.

''John?'' Her soft voice pulled him out of his turbulent thoughts. ''I remember a purple cat.''

John closed his eyes. They hadn't had much the first time they were taken away from their mother, but Celia had had a favorite stuffed animal. A purple cat. Its only adornment was a frayed satin ribbon around his neck.

''Snow White.''

''Snow White?'' Celia's lips tipped in amusement. ''I named a purple cat Snow White?''

''The neighbors had a cat named Snow White, so that's what you named yours.'' John smiled as the long-forgotten memory surfaced once again. The veil of the past lifted and he suddenly had a vivid image of her sleeping on the sofa with one arm wrapped around that stuffed cat.

We don't want to wake Celia up, do we.

Reluctantly, he had left with the social worker…and had not seen Celia again. Until now.

''John?'' Celia stepped forward, tears that had been brimming in her eyes spilling over her perfectly made-up face. ''I think I need a hug from my big brother.''

Chapter Eighteen

"Finn!" Diane opened the door, and the smile of pleasure on her face erased any concern Finn had had about not calling before she stopped by. "I just put on some tea, too. I think that's what you call perfect timing."

"I'm sorry I didn't call first," Finn apologized.

Diane clucked her tongue. "Don't be silly. I've been anxious to talk with you anyway. Neil has taken some time off but he's puttering in the backyard at the moment. Sit down while I get you a cup of tea."

Finn discovered Deborah lying on a colorful patchwork quilt on the floor. She dropped to her knees and picked up Deborah's bare foot, marveling at her perfect toes. "She's getting so big."

"I know. I keep putting away clothes thinking that she'll never grow into them and by the time I put an outfit back on her, it's almost too small." Diane's muffled voice came from the direction of the kitchen. "Here we go."

She swept into the living room and put a wooden

tray on the coffee table, patting one of the cushions on the chintz sofa. "Come sit."

"John went to Celia's last night for dinner with her parents. I haven't talked to Ryan yet, but Celia called this morning and asked him if she could come in after lunch today." Finn picked up one of the cups on the tray and absently sipped the tea. "It's a miracle—them finding each other again after all these years. Something only God could accomplish."

"Maybe this is what John needs," Diane said. "Since D.C., he's been so different somehow. I don't know how to describe it."

Finn felt a slight chill ripple through her. "What happened there?"

"Basically what I told you on the phone," Diane sighed. "They were following a lead that an FBI agent was accepting bribes from a drug dealer. Someone tipped him off and they had to hide out for a few days to stay safe."

To stay alive was what she meant, Finn knew.

"Diane…" Finn read between the lines and knew the men had been through a terrible experience.

"I know, I know." Diane drew a ragged breath. "It shook them both up. Neil told me when they got home that he is done with that part of the investigation. He said he almost went crazy not being able to tell me that he was okay. Thinking that he might never see me or Deborah again. He and John have been offered desk jobs before and always turned them down, but not now. I've always been supportive of Neil's career, but I can't say I'll be upset to have him working from an office from now on."

"And John?" Finn asked.

"Neil said he just went into neutral when they got

back. Maybe finding Celia will help him understand that God is working in his life and that he isn't too far away for miracles.''

''He barely spoke to me yesterday,'' Finn admitted, still feeling the sting of his rejection.

Diane looked at her with affection. ''That's because he's in love with you and he doesn't know how to handle it.''

''What?''

''Finn.'' Diane laughed. ''Don't look so shocked. What is there *not* to love about you?''

''I think I just irritate him.''

''Oh, Finn.'' Diane rose to retrieve Deborah, who had finally managed to tummy-wiggle her way to the edge of the quilt. ''I think that you might confuse him and challenge him, but I doubt that you irritate him.''

''We never did go out for lunch yesterday. Celia and John needed time alone together. I was hoping he'd come in after they'd had a chance to talk, but he just left.''

''Are you driving back today?''

''This afternoon,'' Finn said. ''I'm going to stop back at The Wild Olive to see Ryan first, though.''

As if by unspoken agreement, they turned the conversation to other things, until Neil came in and coaxed Finn outside to see his garden. When Deborah started to yawn and burrow her face into her mother's shoulder, Finn decided it was time to let Diane and Neil put her down for a nap. Diane gave her a warm hug before she left.

''Stop back the next time you're visiting Ryan,'' she called.

''I will,'' Finn promised.

As she neared John's apartment, her foot hovered

above the brake. She saw his car in its parking spot and, wondering why he wasn't at work, impulsively turned her car into the lot and pressed the security button.

"Who is it?"

Finn winced. His tone was far from welcoming. "It's Finn." After several seconds of silence, she heard a *click*.

He was waiting for her in the doorway when she reached the top of the stairs. Almost reluctantly, he stood to the side so she could step into his apartment.

"I suppose you're here because you talked to Celia."

Finn frowned. "No, I've been visiting Diane and Neil."

He looked as if he didn't believe her. "And you haven't spoken to Ryan, either?"

"John, what's going on?" Something in his expression wasn't right. "Did something happen?"

"I had dinner with the Greyson-Fletchers last night," he said. "And then I told Celia that I didn't think it was a good idea if we got involved in each other's lives."

"You did *what?*" Finn cried in disbelief.

He wheeled around and stalked over to the window, putting another six feet of distance between them. "Grow up, Finn. Celia and I have been apart for more than twenty years. You can't expect us to have the relationship that you and Ryan have."

"You're right—not after one dinner together," Finn said. She couldn't believe that he meant what he had just said. "But in time—"

"Do you know what she told me last night? She said that it was okay if I didn't want to have a relationship with her. Then she proceeded to tell me that the most important relationship I could ever have is with the Lord. He loves me. He'll heal the hurts in my past just like He did hers.'' John's eyes narrowed. ''I couldn't believe it. Christians seem to be dropping out of the sky lately!''

Despite his angry words, Finn almost smiled at the obvious frustration in his voice. ''John, please don't shut Celia out of your life. She's your sister.''

''Celia is a stranger,'' John said bluntly. ''My sister was a two-year-old with a runny nose and a dirty face. She wasn't an heiress who lives in a mansion.''

''You don't want to get to know your sister because she has money?'' Finn couldn't believe how stubborn he was being.

''She has everything in the world that I wished for her,'' John said. ''She doesn't need me.''

''I think you're just scared,'' Finn said, seeing the shuttered look on his face. ''She does need you.''

''No one needs me,'' John retorted. ''I don't *want* anyone to need me.''

''I don't know what I'd do without Ryan and the rest of my family, yet you're willing to close everyone out of your life who cares about you,'' Finn said. ''You focus so much on what you don't have, and you don't look at what you do have. John, you have a lot to give.''

The words hung in the air between them.

''And you won't give God a chance, either, because that means you'd have to *love* and that terrifies you, doesn't it.''

''I was wondering when you'd get a sermon in,'' John said disdainfully, turning away from Finn's stricken face. "You and Diane and Celia all out to save my poor soul."

"John…"

"I have to catch a flight out of here in a few hours."

Finn's eyes closed briefly. "So what does this mean?"

John couldn't believe he had to spell it out for her. Why was she putting him through this? Slowly, he pivoted until they were facing each other. "It means I want you to stay out of my life," he said distinctly. "It means that you'll have to turn your missionary tactics on someone else. It means that Diane and Neil have their family, Celia Greyson-Fletcher has hers, you have yours—and you will all *leave me alone*."

"All right," she whispered. "But you can't keep holding up your past like a torch. You may not have had a family growing up, but you can have one now. You can't change the past, but you can start something better. You just don't want to. It's easier this way, isn't it."

John walked over to the door, opened it and waited.

"Goodbye." Finn barely made it to her car before the rush of tears blinded her eyes. She fumbled with the keys and, once inside, leaned her head against the steering wheel and started to pray as the tears fell.

Chapter Nineteen

Finn checked her box one last time before going off duty and started down the hall toward the back room where the lockers were. The door was almost closed, and as she reached out to push it open, she heard her name and paused.

"She's got a week left." It was Wes. "Ten bucks says she doesn't make her probation."

"She hasn't done anything wrong." It was Mike Alloway's lazy drawl.

"She's been messing up reports left and right and there are three reprimands in her file," Wes said. "I say she ain't going to make it."

"Larson likes her," Mike said mildly. "I think she'll do okay."

"You really think she'll make it?"

Carl. Finn bit her lip. She hadn't realized he was at the table with them.

"Hey, you were her training officer," Wes said. "You tell us, smart guy."

"I can't figure women out," Carl said, his voice

changing suddenly. "Sherilynn was happy at home and then she decides to go back to work at that stupid art gallery. The dog gets more attention than I do. I mean, look at Finn. You'd never know by looking at her that she's as selfish as Sherilynn. One of these feminist women who has to have a career to feel important."

Finn was stunned. She had never heard Carl talk like that before. Always he had been encouraging and supportive. And she'd never heard him say a harsh word about his wife.

"Aw, you guys are cavemen," Mike said disgustedly. "That kind of thinking went out with polyester shirts and leisure suits."

"You got a crush on Kelly all of a sudden?" Wes asked.

"She handled that fight last week at the bowling alley like a pro," Mike said. "I always thought I'd hate to have her as my backup, but she jumped right in. By the time it was over, this tough biker was calling her 'ma'am' and thanking her for giving him a ticket for disorderly conduct."

Finn smiled and quietly backed away, leaving the building through the front door. A maple tree in the parking lot was already wearing a patch of scarlet high in its branches. Summer was easing into fall. She had felt the bite in the air when she had gone running with Colin that morning, although the sun still soaked up the chill by noon. She was scheduled for a meeting with Chief Larson next Monday. She had no idea whether she would be asked to leave or continue wearing her badge. And she had been praying fervently for direction. She'd also been spending a lot of time sorting through her decision to make law enforcement her career. How much of it had been to heal the rift between Ryan and their father? Or to bask in her father's approval? How much had been the result of her childish, wide-eyed admiration of John's heroism when he'd saved Seamus?

All her life she'd been protecting people—it came to her as naturally as breathing. But was being a cop the right fit for that desire? That was the question she'd been struggling with. When she had a few years under her belt, maybe she'd be as cynical and jaded as some of the officers she worked with. So far, she'd always counted on her relationship with the Lord to keep her compassionate. To keep her focused.

"Officer Kelly?"

Finn had reached her car and she turned at the sound of a soft voice behind her. Bonnie Lessing was standing several feet away, regarding her shyly. At her side was her daughter, Tina, clutching a piece of paper.

"Mrs. Lessing." Finn crossed the short distance between them. "What can I do for you?"

"I—I just wanted to thank you," the woman stammered, her eyes darting to Finn and then away. "For giving me the name of that lady at the safe house, Sarah. She's been a big help. You probably don't understand, but Jerome hasn't always been like this. I just wanted you to know that me and Tina are going to make a new start. Sarah told me they'd help. I've been getting some counseling."

Finn smiled. "You have a lot of courage, Mrs. Lessing."

The woman returned her smile wanly. "That's funny, Officer Kelly, because I thought that about you when you came to the house that day. I thought to myself, there's a brave woman. I bet she'd never stand still and let a man…you know." Bonnie glanced down at Tina, who was staring up at Finn with wide eyes. "You can give her your picture, honey."

"You drew a picture for me?" Finn bent down and hooked a strand of Tina's dark hair behind her ear. "That was really sweet of you, Tina."

Tina smiled shyly and handed Finn the piece of paper.

"She drew this yesterday at the shelter," Bonnie explained. "And the counselor said she should give it to you."

The drawing was done in childish stick figures. Three people. Two were adults. One was Bonnie, judging by the curly dark hair and glasses. The other was Finn, wearing blue clothing and a huge silver star. The smallest figure was obviously Tina herself, tucked between Finn and her mother. All of their hands were linked.

"I'm going to put it on my refrigerator," Finn said. "How does that sound?"

Tina grinned and nodded vigorously.

"Thank you again," Bonnie said.

"You two take care." Finn took Bonnie's hand and gave it a reassuring squeeze.

Bonnie ruffled her daughter's hair lightly. "We will."

Finn got into her car and carefully put Tina's picture on the passenger seat, then leaned back and closed her eyes.

"That's what You're trying to tell me, isn't it, Lord." she murmured. "That I am making a difference. That I'm in the right place."

When she opened her eyes, she saw Carl Davis emerging from the side door of the department. She slipped out of her car and walked toward him.

"Carl."

He paused as she approached. "Thought you were headed home, Finn."

"I am." Finn met his gaze steadily. "I was getting some things out of my locker and I overheard you guys talking in the break room just now."

She could almost hear Carl's internal rewind button start whirring.

"You asked me to help you out," Carl said, almost defensively. "I thought I could trip up Wes—or even Mike—into admitting that he was making sure you'd mess up your probation. That's all I was doing, Finn. You trusted me to begin with, why the sudden suspicions now?"

"Are you and Sherilynn really having problems?"

Carl laughed. "So I exaggerated a little. Every married couple has some bumpy spots. We're working them out."

Finn was relieved.

"I'd keep an eye on Wes the next few days," Carl advised. "He's pretty convinced you're going to get your walking papers on Monday. He just might do something over the weekend to tip the scales."

"I will. See you tomorrow."

Carl grinned, gave her a comical bow and got into the squad car.

When Finn got home, she let Colin outside and checked the messages on her answering machine. One was from Ryan and the other from her parents. There was nothing from John.

She knew that Celia had been devastated by his decision to keep his distance. Even Diane, who had faithfully confronted him about other issues in the past, had decided the best thing to do was give him some time to work things out.

He's in love with you. Diane's words came back to her and for a moment Finn let them sink roots into her heart. Then she remembered the expression on his face when he told her to leave him alone. The shadows in his eyes had given him away. He was afraid.

Lord, when is he going to realize that love is worth the risk?

John couldn't shake the restless feeling that had hovered over him for several days now, hounding him even in his sleep. He had been glad to be able to go to Mexico on a follow-up for two weeks after telling Finn that he just wanted to be left alone. But he hadn't been prepared for the emptiness that followed. Or the bleakness of his apartment when he returned. Not that it looked bleak anymore. Just the opposite, which made it worse. It was as if Finn's fingerprints were on everything. Even when he slept in the sleigh bed, he remembered the anxious expression on her face as she waited for his approval when he saw it for the first time.

There had been three messages from Celia on his answering machine when he returned, one from Ryan and one from Cole Greyson-Fletcher, Celia's father. He hadn't returned any of them yet. That had been the day before. Now, he paced the confines of his apartment, almost wishing Bradel hadn't forced him to take a few days off after his grueling traveling schedule.

"Think about this for a few days while you try to relax," Bradel had told him. "Hugh Johnson just turned in his resignation because he got an offer to head up security at a private company in Los Angeles.

I need to replace him and you'd be perfect for the job. You'd be in charge of the missing persons division.''

''Neil put you up to this, didn't he?'' John shook his head.

''Yeah, he paid Johnson off so he'd leave and you could take his place,'' Bradel deadpanned. ''Your passion is finding missing people, John. Here's your opportunity to do it, and you wouldn't be doing as much traveling. There's only one thing I'd like you to do if you accept the position, though.''

''Just one?''

Bradel ignored his sarcasm. ''Here's a person I'd like you to call.'' He fished in his pocket and pulled out a blue business card. ''I made a few calls. This doctor is one of the best.''

John stared at the words printed on the card. ''Why now?''

''I've known you a long time,'' Bradel answered. ''I went along with your argument that your disability made you a better undercover operative. Now that you won't be doing that kind of work anymore, it's not necessary for you to limit the things you can do. Too much of a sacrifice for your job, I always thought.''

Too much too fast, John thought. ''I don't remember agreeing to take the position.''

Bradel grinned. ''If you don't take it, I'm going to give it to Neil Wallace.''

''The Neil Wallace who deleted half our files last year when he was trying to find eBay?''

''That's the guy,'' Bradel said cheerfully. ''Think about it, John. I'll see you in my office in a few days.''

Bradel knew exactly which buttons to push, John thought, replaying their conversation. That was why he was the head of the agency. And he wasn't surprised

Neil was going to pressure him to accept the position. When they had been huddled in the basement of that crack house in D.C., Neil had muttered that they were getting too old for the cloak-and-dagger stuff. Silently, John had agreed with him.

The telephone rang, and even though he was standing two feet away, he let the machine answer for him.

"John." It was Diane. He hadn't talked to her or Neil since his return. *"If you're there, please pick up the phone. I wanted to tell you that Ryan is having a surprise birthday party for Finn on Saturday and he wants you to come. Call me for the details. 'Bye."*

It was Thursday. Why wouldn't they leave him in peace? For a moment, his hand hovered over the phone. He wanted to call Ryan and tell him that under no circumstances was he going to Finn's party, but then he realized Celia might answer the phone if she was working. His hand dropped to his side in defeat. He just wouldn't show up. They would all figure out why.

The business card for the doctor who specialized in prosthetics fluttered to the floor.

You can still sweep a girl off her feet. Finn's words came back to him with the momentum of a freight train. Is that what he'd done? Swept her off her feet? He was ten years older than her, for crying out loud. He pictured her curled up in the oversize chair, sipping the tea he'd made for her. Wearing the T-shirt that said to protect and to serve. She was so willing to step into the gaps. The night at the Kelly bonfire she had positioned herself in front of him and Ryan, shielding them from her family's enthusiasm about law enforcement. Then she'd waded into the middle of a domestic situation without backup. They were in the same line of work, and yet Finn didn't lock away a part of herself like he did. She was one of the few cops he'd met who brought everything she was into her job—her faith, her values, even her feelings.

John bent down and picked up the business card.

Her probation meeting was coming up soon. And who was protecting Finn? She was being ambushed by someone in her own department and he'd purposefully pulled out. That's what he seemed to be good at. He'd almost turned it into an art.

She has someone to watch her back. Carl Davis. And she has to learn she can't passively stand by and watch while someone deliberately sabotages her career.

And God. Finn would say He was watching out for her, too.

Somewhere in the Scriptures, he knew that God was called a shepherd.

"I just want You to know," John said out loud. "That one of Your lambs might be in trouble. You may want to stay close."

The restless feeling that dogged him throughout the evening followed him into the night. He tried to attribute it to the decisions he needed to make about his job, but his thoughts kept turning back to Finn. He lay awake, staring at the ceiling, and tried to block her face from his mind.

He couldn't love her. Wouldn't love her. He'd seen Neil's anguished face when they thought they weren't going to make it back. He'd heard him praying softly to God to strengthen Diane and watch over Deborah. There was no way he could love someone like that and risk losing them. He'd already lost enough. He'd done the best thing for Finn when he'd told her to stay out of his life.

The best for her...or for you?

John scowled in the darkness at the thought. The best for both of them, even though Finn wouldn't agree. She'd actually accused him of being afraid to love. Finn's words from their last conversation pierced him.

You can't change the past, but you can start something better. You just don't want to. It's easier this way, isn't it?

"Why did you bring her into my life, God?" He hurled the words at the ceiling in frustration and suddenly remembered the day he'd teased Finn that maybe he was an answer to her prayer. "What do you want me to do?"

Go back to her.

Those four simple words sliced like steel through his churning thoughts. He sat up in bed and looked at the clock. Four in the morning. This was crazy. To drive back to Miranda Station without calling first. To show up out of the blue after he'd told her to stay out of his life…

Weighed down with a sense of urgency he couldn't explain, he questioned his sanity even as he got dressed and searched for his car keys.

He had to go back.

Chapter Twenty

Finn returned from her morning run and glanced at the clock. It was still early. Not even nine yet. She was thankful she was working the afternoon shift because it would give her the time to run to the grocery store for a few things and pot some mums for Anne. Her parents had called the evening before and told her they were coming to take her out for a birthday dinner on the weekend. As anxious as she was to see them, she didn't feel much like celebrating. Two weeks had gone by without a word from John. For all her fervent prayers on his behalf, it looked as though he was going to stubbornly hold to his plan not to have anything to do with the people who cared about him. Ryan had told her during their last conversation that he recognized a man who was running from God. He'd tried it once himself.

Celia kept in close contact with her for which Finn was thankful. The two of them were becoming close friends. The bond they shared in Christ lent a deepness to their growing relationship that Finn treasured.

"Colin, I'm going out to the range," Finn said impulsively. She needed something more demanding than grocery shopping to take her mind off John Gabriel. Retrieving her gun from its locked case, she was almost ready to walk out the door when the telephone rang. The temptation to ignore it was strong. Sighing, she crossed the room to pick it up.

Minutes later, she was in her car, headed toward the industrial park several miles outside the city limits.

You should have brought your radio, she scolded herself. In her haste, she had left her police radio in its charger next to the bed. And her gun was still on the kitchen table. She had forgotten that, too. For a moment, she wondered if she should just drive to the department and talk to Chief Larson, then decided against it. With her probation hanging in the balance, this just might be the thing that would result in getting her walking papers. She'd just check out the old building and make sure nothing was amiss.

When she got out of the car, there was no sign of anyone. The old creamery was on the edge of the industrial park, standing knee high in a field of yellow grass. Cautiously, she walked up to the front door. It had been boarded shut to keep people from trespassing, and was still intact. Finn scanned the front of the building. The windows on the first floor were boarded up, but the windows on the second floor had become prime targets for vandals over the years and only jagged glass teeth remained wedged in the frames. She walked around the side of the building, looking for signs of forced entry. Her heart kicked suddenly as she noticed one of the side doors hanging limply on its hinge.

Finn climbed inside.

She heard a *snap* not far away and quietly made her

way down the dim hall. The place was a labyrinth of rooms and corridors. When she rounded a corner, she saw a man watching a thread of fire creep up the wall. A can of gasoline was on the floor beside him. As if sensing her presence, he turned suddenly in her direction. It was Ricky Calhoun.

"Ricky! No!" Finn started toward him.

He jumped back, staring at her with an almost comical expression of disbelief. He dropped the lighter he'd been holding and took off running in the opposite direction. Already the fire was eating its way through a pile of rags on the floor. Finn dodged it and doggedly followed Ricky.

"Come back here," she yelled. "You have to get out of the building."

Ignoring her, he clattered up a flight of steps.

"Ricky!" Finn paused to listen. She didn't know how long it would take for the fire to get a firm hold on the building. Part of her wanted to go for help, but she knew Ricky was scared and she needed to make sure he was clear of the building. She followed him up the stairs.

A door was still quivering when she reached the second floor. Finn pulled it open and instinctively took a step forward, but then stopped abruptly. In this particular room, the floor had caved in, leaving a crisscross of exposed beams. Ricky was inching his way across one of them, heading toward a narrow window ledge on the other side.

"Ricky, you're going to fall. This place isn't safe...."

The wild-eyed look he shot her over his shoulder was the only evidence he'd heard her. Finn stepped

onto the beam, clutching the door frame with one hand.
"I'm going to leave, Ricky. You can come back now."

With a loud creak of protest against the weight of
his body, the rafter suddenly shifted beneath his feet
and tipped him over the side. Ricky screamed. The
beam snapped in half. Finn lunged toward the wooden
door frame but felt her fingers slide down the length
of it. There was nothing to hold on to. She felt herself
falling...and then her world went black.

Ricky's groaning stirred her back to consciousness.
She tried to blink away the fuzziness that surrounded
everything.

"My leg," Ricky gasped. He lay several feet away
from her, his face contorted with pain. "I think it's
broken."

Finn forced herself to concentrate. She pushed herself into a sitting position and looked around the room
into which they'd fallen. The room was small but the
walls were made of brick. They were in the original
part of the creamery. Smoke was already collecting in
a light haze above them.

Finn pulled herself to Ricky's side and put her hand
on his arm, sucking in her breath at the sharp, stabbing
pain that radiated through her chest. Little sharp points
of light danced in front of her eyes. She could hear the
popping and snapping of the fire as it worked its way
relentlessly through the building toward them. They
didn't have much time. The door was boarded up. Finn
noticed a huge piece of metal tacked to the wall on one
side of the room and she crawled over to it, her whole
body tingling with pain. The white lights were brighter
now and it was getting more and more difficult to blink
them away. She grasped the piece of metal and pulled.

There was a crawl space behind it. That might offer some shelter.

"You have to get in here, Ricky."

"I can't move." Ricky closed his eyes and pressed his lips together in a tight seam.

"I'll help you."

He shrieked in pain as she looped her arm through his, half dragged him to the crawl space and pushed him inside.

"I'm going to cover up the opening with this again," Finn whispered. "You have to make noise when you hear the fire fighters. Do you understand me?"

Ricky's eyes opened and they were glazed with fear, but he nodded. "Where will you be? Don't leave me here."

"I won't," Finn promised. "I'll be out here. But remember, you have to make noise."

She pushed the metal sheet back in place and carefully positioned herself against it. Someone must have seen the smoke by now and called the fire department. They still had a chance. If the fire was put out before the smoke filled up the room, they had a chance.

Lord, send someone. Finn dropped her head on her knees and felt the pain subside slightly. The little white lights became a wave that washed over her. She sighed and let them carry her away.

The door to Finn's house wasn't locked and, after knocking several times, John let himself in. Colin danced excitedly around his feet.

"Hey, boy." John scratched the dog absently behind his ears as he looked around. Seamus had been out, but Anne was sure Finn was home. The faint smell of cloves and ginger still hung in the air. She must have been burning a candle again. A garland of silk autumn leaves and bittersweet was wound around the curtain rod.

''Finn?'' He called her name again and figured she was in the backyard. He started to walk through the house and that's when he spotted her gun on the table. The clip was sitting next to it on the table and the trigger lock was off. He frowned, knowing she was usually careful with her weapon. He picked it up and turned it over in his hand. A short, shrill beep caught his attention and he walked over to her answering machine. Without thinking, he pressed the button. Apparently Finn had reached the phone and picked it up at the same time the machine did, so it recorded her entire conversation. John started to walk away, but then went completely still as he listened to the words exchanged between Finn and Carl Davis, her training officer.

''Finn, did I get you away from something?''

''Just going out to the range for an hour. What's going on?''

''You know that hunch you had about the fires? Well, I think you may be onto something. I saw your little friend by the old creamery when I was on my way home just now. Thought maybe you'd want to check it out. Be careful, though, you know who his old man is.''

''Thanks, Carl. I'll take care of it.''

The whole conversation struck John as odd. Why had Davis mentioned the fires? And if there was someone suspicious that needed to be checked out, why call Finn at home when she was obviously off duty? Why not call the department and send someone else? John raced out the door and right over to Chief's house.

''Where is the old creamery?'' he asked, startling

Anne as he burst into the kitchen without knocking first.

"It's out of town about half a mile," Anne said. "Near the industrial park. Did you find Finn?"

"No." John ran his hand through his hair.

"Is something wrong, John?" Anne asked, a worried look on her face.

"I hope not," John muttered, but a feeling of dread swept over him, so powerful that his legs felt leaden as he headed out the door again.

The creamery was an ancient bastion of wood and brick. Now it stood, abandoned, as a lonely testament to an earlier age. When John pulled up, he could already see curls of smoke rolling out of a broken window. He punched in some numbers on his cell phone and then ran toward the building.

"Finn!" He yelled her name but didn't really expect to get a response. Her Jeep was parked near the building and somehow he knew she was still inside the structure. Within minutes, sirens filled the air as police cruisers and fire trucks wound their way to the scene.

Chief Larson climbed out of an unmarked squad and made his way over to John's side.

"I think Finn's still inside the building," John said without preamble.

"Are you sure?" Larson's heavy brows came together.

"Her car's there but there's no sign of her," John said. "Were there any other 911 calls placed?"

"Only one after yours," Larson said. "Someone down the road who saw the smoke."

"No one could survive in there."

John heard the muttered words behind him. He stared at the billowing smoke and heard the creak and groan of the building as part of it began to succumb to the blaze. Fortunately, the brick was slowing the fire down.

Wes came over and stood next to him, his face carved out of stone. "Is there anything you want me to do?" he asked John tersely.

"I want you to get Finn's dog and bring him back here," John said. "And have someone pick up Carl Davis."

Word about the fire was spreading. Even off-duty officers began to arrive to see if they could provide any assistance. In his entire career, John had never felt so helpless. All he could do was watch as the firefighters fought to get control of the fire.

Wes finally arrived with Colin, who whined and pulled on the leash.

"Just a few more minutes," John murmured. "Then we can go in."

"Let the fire department handle this," Larson said, putting his hand on John's shoulder.

John stepped away. "I'm going in to help them look."

"We're all going in," Wes said.

Their eyes met, and John nodded. Colin brushed against him impatiently and whined. "Okay, boy, let's find Finn."

Slowly the group of men picked their way through the rubble. The smoke had cleared somewhat but timbers had given way, toppling into charred heaps on the floor. Colin strained at the leash.

Wes met John at a turn in the hall. "No sign of her. Watch your step, Gabriel."

Each minute that ticked away added to the horrible

weight in John's chest. Finally, he let go of Colin's leash. "Find her."

Colin streaked down the corridor, dodging debris as John tried to keep up with him. Up a flight of stairs to the second level. Colin whined outside a door that had been partially burned away, although it didn't seem as if the fire had had a grip on that part of the building for too long.

John peered inside. "She's not…"

Colin whined again.

John nudged the door open with his foot and looked down. His vision blurred suddenly as he saw her below him, sitting against a wall, her hair a bright spot of color. He couldn't see her face because her head was resting on her knees. There was something in the relaxed stillness of her body that sent fear spiraling through him. Maybe the smoke…

"Finn!"

No movement. The smoke burned his eyes and made it difficult to breathe. Colin let out a series of sharp, warning barks, and John heard voices coming toward them.

"We've got to find a way down there," he rasped.

Within seconds, one of the firefighters called to him. "Down here."

They broke through the door that had been boarded shut and John made his way to her side. When he reached her, he dropped to his knees and his hand shook violently as he lifted her head. Seconds behind him were the paramedics.

Her eyes were closed.

"Finn? It's John. Can you hear me, honey?" A faint pulse beat beneath his questing fingers but there was no response from her.

"Sir." It was a paramedic. "Let us take a look at her."

Reluctantly, he allowed the paramedic to begin an assessment of her vital signs. "Better get a board down here. There's swelling behind her left ear and it's draining clear fluid," the paramedic said crisply to his partner. "Let's get her stabilized."

John heard a low moan. Unbelievably, it came from behind the metal grate where Finn had been sitting. He pulled the cover aside and saw a young man stuffed in the space behind it.

"Calhoun." Chief Larson knelt beside John, his expression grim. "I can't wait to hear the story behind this one. Wes! Get Calhoun on the phone and tell him his kid's at St. Elizabeth's. And get another paramedic down here."

The young man's eyes flickered open. "My leg is broken."

At that particular moment, realizing this was probably the arsonist the fire department had been trying to catch for months, John could have cheerfully broken his other one. "You'll be all right."

"She told me to make noise," Ricky said slowly, his eyes still dull with pain. A cough racked his body.

John's jaw clamped shut. He suddenly realized what Finn had discovered earlier. The small cubby she had shoved him into had a direct link to the fresh air outside. He could see daylight shining through a pipe. Finn had deliberately put him there, knowing he wouldn't be overcome by smoke if they were found in time. And she had positioned herself right in front of him. A human marker.

"We're ready to go." One of the paramedics paused

and looked at John. ''Would you like to ride along with her?''

John nodded. ''Has someone called the Kellys?''

''I did,'' Wes said. ''They're meeting us at St. E's. I'll drop the dog off at home, too.''

John got in the back of the ambulance and reached out to take Finn's hand. ''What's wrong with her?'' John asked, bracing himself for the worst.

The paramedics exchanged looks. ''We can only discuss her condition with family,'' one of them said apologetically.

Family. And that, John thought bitterly, was the greatest irony of all. He'd told her he didn't want a family. He'd chosen to be an outsider and now he'd gotten his wish. He was being treated like one.

Chapter Twenty-One

Within hours, the surgeon had called a family meeting. Ryan was already there, with Celia at his side. Seamus, pale but stoic, had a bracing arm around Anne's waist. Finn's parents were on their way to the hospital.

Ryan paused and looked back as they filed into the family lounge. "John, you are welcome to come with us."

John didn't hesitate. He followed them and took a seat beside Celia, who looked so broken that he instinctively reached out and took her hand. She scooted closer and leaned against his shoulder.

"When Finn fell, she suffered a skull fracture," the surgeon told them. "There is swelling on her brain and a small amount of bleeding. She hasn't regained consciousness since she fell."

"She wasn't unconscious right after she fell," John said without thinking.

Everyone looked at him.

"What do you mean?" The surgeon frowned

slightly. "I was told the paramedics found her unconscious."

"She was awake long enough to save someone's life in that building," John said. "The arsonist has already given the police a statement. Finn fell but then she pulled him into an area where he would be safe until help arrived."

The surgeon shook his head slowly. "I don't think that's likely, given the nature of her injuries. She wouldn't have been in any condition to assist another injured person. That would have been—"

"Impossible?" Ryan voiced the question.

"I don't discount what this young man said in his statement, but I understand he was suffering from shock as well as a broken leg. It could be that he imagined the scenario he gave you."

"What would it mean if he hadn't?" Seamus asked.

"If she was conscious after the fall and making decisions—talking—then that would be a very good sign," he admitted. "It would mean that the young lady is a fighter and she's going to need to be. She's still unconscious and it's hard to predict when she'll wake up, but she's young and healthy. I will caution you, however, that she is considered critical at this point."

John felt Celia's fingers convulse in his. Anne buried her face against Seamus's shoulder.

"When can we see her?" Ryan asked.

"Probably this evening." The surgeon's gaze swept over each one of them. "It seems you've already experienced one blessing today. It wouldn't hurt to start praying for another one."

The blast from a handgun shattered the air.

"John?"

Ryan was walking toward him. Alone, thank goodness. John didn't know if he could face both Ryan and his sister at the moment. Anger welled up inside of him and he directed it at the nearest target—Finn's brother.

"So this is how God takes care of people who love Him?" John threw the question at Ryan as he got closer. He wanted to believe that God was good, that He didn't set out to harm His children, but the fire had brought all the doubts back.

"God is taking care of Finn."

John aimed at the target and fired again, but Ryan didn't flinch.

"Sure, that's why she's lying in a hospital bed fighting for her life—" He bit off the words and reloaded.

"The fire chief said that if she hadn't fallen into that particular room, she would have died," Ryan said.

"She still might," John said, his voice tight.

"She might." Tears formed in his eyes even as he agreed.

"She put that punk kid's life above her own. On *purpose!* Why would she even think that he was more important than her? She never *thought.* She just acted out of that senseless faith she clings to."

"You did the same thing for Seamus. You put your life on the line for him."

"Seamus is a good man. An honorable man. Not some loser who gets his kicks lighting fires." John couldn't believe Ryan could even compare the two situations. He'd had nothing but respect for Seamus.

"She did the right thing. She did what she promised to do when she became a police officer," Ryan argued quietly. "But more than that, she tries to do what God calls her to do."

"The right thing?" John spun around and faced him, unable to believe that Ryan thought Finn had done the right thing when she'd risked her life for Ricky Calhoun. "Saving that little weasel was the *right* thing to do?"

"You don't know my sister at all, do you." Now anger was reflected in Ryan's eyes. "You think she has a senseless faith. Finn would tell you that her faith is the only thing that makes sense. She lives what she believes…and is one of the few people who do. I'm proud of her—" Ryan's voice broke and they stared at each other.

"There's a story in the Old Testament about three men who were told they had to worship the golden image the king had commanded them to worship, or else they'd be thrown into a fire. They refused to do it, saying that God was able to save them from the fire if He chose, but if He didn't save them, it didn't matter. They knew they were making the right decision. When they were thrown into the fire, suddenly the king saw four men standing in the blaze instead of three. Don't you see, John, Finn knows that whatever happens in her life—the good and the bad—God is there with her."

He remembered the first time he'd spent time with Finn and she'd thanked God for both the joys and the challenges that came into her life.

"Celia is worried about you," Ryan said, changing the subject. "Come back with me."

John nodded wearily.

They drove in silence back to Seamus's house, where the Kellys were beginning to gather. "Are you staying?" Ryan asked.

"Yes." *Just try to get me to leave.*

"Come on." Ryan opened the door to Finn's house, where Colin was waiting for them.

"She always saw the hero inside that dog." There was a half smile on Ryan's face as he looked down at Colin.

She said she saw the hero in me, too. God, why was I so stupid? How could I have been so arrogant? Told her that she wasn't strong? Wasn't courageous?

Ryan pushed something into his hand, and when he looked down he saw it was Finn's Bible.

"I suggest you take some time and get to know my sister—and her Savior," Ryan suggested softly.

"How?"

Ryan tapped the book. "Just start reading. You'll figure it out."

"I don't have your faith."

"Faith is a gift that God helps you open."

John stayed up until two in the morning, sifting through the passages that Finn had highlighted in blue. It was amazing. She had notes scrawled in margins, dated answers to prayers. Sometimes, she had simply drawn a heart next to a verse that must have meant something to her.

When he found his name written next to a passage in Isaiah, he laid his head down on the Bible and cried out to God, finally giving in to the things that had tormented him for so long.

"I have summoned you by name, you are mine.
When you pass through the waters, I will be with you;
And when you pass through the rivers, they will not sweep over you.

When you walk through the fire, you will not be
burned...
For I am the Lord your God.''

Finn had written the words ''John—a promise'' underneath the verses.

*You promised, but I was still burned. I did walk
through the fire—these scars prove it. And what about
Finn?*

''I have summoned you by name.''

What about Finn?

''I will be with you.''

There was a light knock on the door. Colin, resting
at John's feet, thumped his tail. When John opened the
door, Ryan and Celia were standing on the porch. He
didn't even need to ask why they were there.

''You gave this Bible to Finn, didn't you.''

Ryan sat down in the chair. ''When she was twelve,
she surrendered her life to the Lord. I had the privilege
of praying with her.''

''Maybe you could tell me what you said.''

Chapter Twenty-Two

Finn opened her eyes, aware of a dull ache radiating through her entire body. She tried to focus on the interior of the room and realized she was in the hospital. There was an IV attached to the back of her hand, the tube connected to a pole beside the bed. What had happened? Dimly, her memory began to return, piecing the fragments together until she had a blurry memory of finding Ricky Calhoun in the creamery and following him. And there was fire. They both fell. She'd heard voices and felt herself being lifted. Tilting her head slightly, she was stunned when her gaze fell on John, sound asleep in the chair next to the bed.

His head rested awkwardly against the vinyl back and a thick layer of stubble shadowed the lower half of his face. The lines that fanned out from the corners of his eyes seemed more pronounced.

She tried to say his name but all that came out was a tiny gasp. Instantly, his eyes snapped open and he sat up, staring at her.

"Finn."

She watched the weariness stamped on his face give way to amazement. And then relief. He put his arm around her and buried his face against her neck. She could only lie there helplessly as his body shook with emotion and she felt the warmth of his tears on her skin. Mustering all her strength, she patted him on the back.

"I should have fallen through the floor a month ago," she rasped, testing her voice. "And by the way…who poured hot gravel down my throat?"

"You were on a ventilator," John explained. "That's why your throat is sore."

A ventilator? Wasn't that the contraption that breathed for a person when they couldn't? *What happened to me, Lord?*

"I've got to get your parents. And Seamus and Anne are here, too," John said. He rose stiffly to his feet and rubbed his back. The expression on his face brought tears to her own eyes.

"They're here?"

"You'll get all your questions answered," John promised. "But first I have to track down some people who are going to want to know you're awake."

Finn closed her eyes again, feeling incredibly weak. When the door opened again, a nurse bustled up to her, all smiles.

"Miss Kelly, glad you decided to join us."

"How long have I been in the hospital?"

"Almost ten days," the nurse said briskly. "I'm going to check your vitals now, before the doctor comes in to say hello."

"Ten days!" Finn croaked in disbelief.

"That's right. I'll get Dr. Elliott down here now.

He's been anxious to see what color your eyes are.'' She winked.

Over the next hour, people came and went with quiet precision. Dr. Elliott, a young man with tousled blond hair and tiny gold-framed glasses, sat on the end of her bed and explained she had had a skull fracture resulting from the fall. The fracture had caused bleeding on her brain. He was going to schedule her for another CAT scan to make sure everything was, in his words, ''where it should be.'' Finn tried to follow everything he said but finally her eyelids fluttered and Dr. Elliott laughed.

''Okay, I take it as a personal insult when I bore a pretty girl and she can't stay awake. The bottom line here, Finn, is that your recovery is going to go uphill from now on. You might need some physical therapy depending on how eager your brain is to give directions to the rest of your body, but don't worry if you don't remember things right away. It'll all come back.''

He paused in the hallway, where an anxious group of people waited for the opportunity to see her. ''She's a lucky young lady,'' he said. ''Very lucky.''

''I'm sorry, Doctor,'' Ryan said. ''But we don't believe in luck.''

Dr. Elliott smiled. ''Neither do I. You can go in now, but don't tire her too much. She's still on meds for the pain and she's going to be drifting in and out for a while.''

When they had weaned her off some of the stronger drugs and removed the ventilator, Dr. Elliott hadn't been able to tell them just how long it would be before Finn would wake up on her own. The swelling in her brain had subsided and the EEG test had shown normal brain activity. He had said it would just be a question of time, and now, less than six hours later, she was awake. It wasn't difficult to see the evidence of God's power in room 214.

"Finn." Seamus sighed. "You gave us quite a scare."

"Dr. Elliott says I'll be fine," Finn reassured them. "In fact, he thinks I may be able to go home by the end of the week. How is Colin holding up?"

"He misses you," Anne said. "But John has been staying at your house taking care of him since your accident."

"All this time?" Finn asked in surprise.

Seamus and Anne exchanged glances, but all Anne said was, "We've been given strict instructions by your young doctor not to tire you out, sweetheart. We just had to see with our own eyes that you're all right."

"We'll be back this evening," Seamus promised, giving her an awkward kiss. He turned away, but not before Finn saw tears in his eyes.

The next people to sneak in were Ryan and her parents, their faces mirroring their relief at seeing her sitting up in bed, poking at a bowl of red gelatin on a tray.

"Hey, sis." Ryan bent down and brushed a kiss on top of her head.

"You've been praying," she whispered.

The tears that began to leak out of his eyes spoke volumes. "Me and a whole lot of others," he said quietly. "Finn, you'll never know how close—"

"I think I do," Finn interrupted, managing to smile. Dr. Elliott hadn't come right out and said it, but she had gathered that her prognosis hadn't been good in the beginning.

She talked with her parents briefly, until fatigue

started to roll in like an evening fog. "I think that the nurse slipped something into my Jell-O."

"We'll be back," Nolan Kelly said. "Love you." He dropped a kiss on her forehead.

"Love you, too." *Where is John?* she wanted to ask, but everyone had already slipped out of the room.

By the next morning she was feeling stronger. The same nurse who had been on the floor the day before was back again. She opened the drapes.

"Can you get up for a few moments, Miss Kelly?"

"I'd like to try," Finn said.

"I understand there's a show starting in a few minutes that you won't want to miss." She smiled at Finn and helped her out of bed. With the nurse's arm at Finn's waist to steady her, they moved slowly to the chair next to the window.

Finn looked down and gasped. A line of squad cars was parked just outside, lining the street next to the hospital. The red-and-blue lights made slow, sweeping patterns over the lawn.

"I think your friends are saying hello." The nurse grinned. "Sit down for a minute or two." She tucked a blanket around Finn's legs just as the door opened and John stepped into the room.

He glanced at Finn, then at the nurse. "Ready?"

She nodded, and John motioned to someone in the hall. Chief Larson came in first, followed by Captain Mitchell. Their arms were brimming with long-stemmed roses. Blue roses. The rest of the Miranda Station Police Department was right behind them, filling the small room with a field of blue. One by one, they stepped up to Finn and offered her a word of encouragement and gave her a flower.

Wes paused in front of her. "Hurry up and get back to work," he finally said gruffly. "You got a lot of guts, Kelly, I'll say that much."

Finn gave a gurgle of laughter. "That's high praise, Wes."

He reddened a little and then squeezed her hand. "Take it easy. And by the way—congratulations. I heard you made your probation."

"Quite a tribute," the nurse said, her eyes misty, as the men filed out again.

Finn brushed her face against the roses and inhaled their fragrance.

The nurse smiled at John. "I'll be back."

"Blue roses are rare," John said. "I heard they had to come from out of state."

"Tell me what happened." Finn looked up at him, waiting.

"Are you sure you're ready?"

John walked over and sat on the edge of her bed, not daring to get any closer. Just seeing her gray eyes looking into his the day before, when he wasn't sure he'd ever see them again, had completely decimated his self-control. He hadn't even been able to come back, not knowing if he'd break down and blubber like a baby again at the sight of her.

"It was Carl Davis who was trying to get you fired," John said, watching her expression carefully to gauge her reaction. As the words sunk in, Finn's eyes darkened.

"Carl?"

"I found the message on your answering machine when I got to your house that day. It didn't make sense, him calling you like that when he should have notified the department or checked it out himself. He'd been driving by the creamery and recognized Ricky Calhoun hanging around the building. Apparently, Davis figured that by telling you he'd seen Calhoun there, you'd get in hot water for accusing him of being involved in the fires. That would have sealed your termination on Monday. He hadn't figured that you were right all along about that kid. He thought you'd call the fire department or the P.D., not go there alone.''

"Why?"

He knew what she was asking. "I talked to Davis myself. He was having problems with his marriage because of his wife's career choices. She was starting to hint about getting a divorce and he was getting pretty bitter. He started transferring his anger to you, doing malicious things that made him feel like he still had some control over something in his life.''

Finn closed her eyes. "And Ricky?"

"Out on bond already, thanks to good old dad," John said. "He wants to see you, but so far no one has given him permission.''

"I want to see him," Finn murmured.

He had known she'd say that. "I'll let him know."

"According to Wes, there's a rumor that I made my probation.''

John asked God to help him find the right words. It was a whole new experience for him. "Finn, no one would blame you if you didn't go back. Anyone that went through what you did would think twice about pinning on their badge again.''

He saw Finn look at his empty sleeve. It figured.

"You did."

He couldn't deny it. "That's because the uniform goes all the way through." It was something Seamus had said to him a long time ago, but he hadn't remembered it until now.

Finn's brow knit together. "God used me to save someone's life. I'm not going to quit now."

"Ricky."

"No. Someone else. When you go back to my house tonight, look on the refrigerator." Her gray eyes lifted to his face. "Why were you at my house that day?"

John stood up abruptly. That was the line of questioning he wasn't ready for. "You look tired. I'll get those flowers off your lap so you can get back into bed."

"What will happen to Carl?"

It was so like Finn to do welfare checks on everyone, he thought in amazement. He could see the forgiveness already warming her eyes. "He's on leave at the moment until this all gets sorted out."

"He didn't mean for me to get trapped in the building."

"No." John couldn't deny that, but a shudder rippled through him as his mind replayed those moments at the creamery. "Did you know that Colin found you?"

"Colin?" No one had told her that.

"He passed that test with flying colors," John said. "He found you within minutes."

Finn smiled to herself. Her maverick shepherd had become a hero. "Give him an extra bone for me."

"It's already been done." John gathered up the roses and set them down on the table. "I'll call the nurse to help you."

"You can help me."

A muscle worked in John's jaw, but he slipped his arm around her and nudged her onto the bed. "Okay?"

Why wouldn't he look at her? "John?"

"I'll be back later." He escaped silently from the room.

Later that day, a dozen white roses were added to the ones from the officers. Every petal was soft and perfectly formed. With trembling fingers, Finn opened the card and read the inscription.

To Finn, the Courageous One.

The card wasn't signed.

Courageous One. That was what her very Irish name meant, but she was amazed that he'd known that.

"Finn doesn't understand why you won't come to see her."

John looked up from where he sat on the sofa and saw Celia standing in the doorway. As always, she looked serene and beautiful. Her pale-green linen shift accentuated the color of her eyes and a modest diamond cross on a delicate chain was her only adornment. He leaned back and rubbed his eyes.

"I don't know what to say to her."

"Try something simple like 'I love you.'"

John groaned. "If that's your idea of simple, I'd hate to hear complicated."

"I don't hear you denying it." She sat down beside him and reached for his hand, searching his eyes.

"I'm not. But do you realize she almost died because of me?"

"How did you come up with that?"

He narrowed his eyes but didn't pull his hand away.

Celia looked at him calmly, obviously unintimidated by his sudden glower.

"If I had let myself think about it—about *her*—I would have figured out it was Davis. I reached for the easiest suspect because I wanted to be done with Finn Kelly. Instead of helping her, I suggested she find someone she could trust to help her out—Carl Davis. The guy she picked was the one who was trying to destroy her career. I could have been more involved, but I let her go it alone. If I hadn't come back here that day…"

"John, make sure you aren't using guilt as your reason to stay away from Finn now," Celia cautioned softly. "You can always come up with a thousand reasons not to love someone."

"She deserves someone better."

"That's two," Celia admonished. "You've got nine hundred and ninety-eight left."

"You are a pest," John growled. "You were a pest when you were two and you haven't changed a bit."

Celia actually giggled. "She's coming home the day after tomorrow. All the Kellys are converging at Seamus's. They say it's a belated birthday party for Finn, but all they really want to do is hug her and see for themselves that she's all right."

"Does Finn know?"

Celia immediately guessed what he meant. "That you've given your life to the Lord? We think you should be the one to tell her."

"I feel like I'm in the kindergarten class for believers."

"Everyone starts there," Celia said with a smile. "And it looks to me like you're a willing student."

She touched the new leather Bible on the sofa between them. "Nine hundred and ninety-seven."

"All right, I'll be at the party!"

Celia stood up. "I'm going to find Ryan and tell him."

"Any idea when *he's* going to stop running?"

Celia whirled around and then relaxed when she saw the teasing glint in his eyes. "You aren't the only man who can come up with a thousand reasons," she said simply.

Chapter Twenty-Three

When Finn got out of her parents' car, the yard was filled with balloons in honor of her homecoming. Colin even sported a bright bandanna around his neck. When he saw her, he began to bark furiously and execute perfect figure-eights around her legs. Finn knelt down and wrapped her arms around the thick ruff of fur on his neck.

"Hey, buddy," she murmured. "I guess you saved me, too, huh? Now we're even."

Most of her family was there, unfolding like a banner across the yard as they moved toward her. Even Neil and Diane Avery had come, at Ryan's invitation. Finn scanned the faces and felt a sharp stab of disappointment when she realized that John wasn't part of her welcoming party. What had she expected? He hadn't told her what had brought him back to Miranda Station the day of the fire. When she'd asked Ryan if John was planning to come to the party, her brother had reluctantly told her that John had gone back to

Chicago and that he wasn't sure what John's plans were.

But he'd rested his head on her chest and cried when she'd opened her eyes for the first time. She replayed that memory at least a hundred times a day.

But he's not here now. He hasn't stopped running away.

As the day wore on, Finn was humbled by the fact that the party was so much more than a celebration of her birthday—it was a celebration of God's faithfulness. Even for those who were skeptical, there was no denying that something wondrous had taken place when she was found alive in the wreckage of that burned-out building. She even sensed a softening in her father as he took her hand at one point and told her that there had to be something going on during all those prayers they had said for her.

She was treated like a fragile porcelain doll for the rest of the day, stuffed with cake and given gifts to open...until the weariness began to seep back into her and her mother graciously brought the party to a close.

When Ryan found Celia in the kitchen, she was washing up the last of the dishes and putting things away. Noisily. Gently, he reached out and took a very large cake knife from her hand.

"He promised he'd be here," Celia said. "Finn was crushed. Oh, she tried to hide it, but I could tell."

"He'll be here."

"In case you haven't noticed, the party is over. Finn is exhausted and everyone is going home." Celia made a grab for the knife, but Ryan only grinned.

"Oh no, you don't. Did you know your eyes flash like emeralds when you're angry?" he tossed.

"Is this an example of the blarney I hear the Irish are experts at dishing out?" Celia said tartly, but she couldn't stop herself from smiling.

"Knowing John like I'm beginning to, I'd say this is exactly the time he'll show up. He needs to see Finn alone."

Celia considered that. "You might be right."

"He hasn't been to the hospital since the day after she woke up. In the past week he's become a believer and struggled with some pretty tough questions. I know, because I'm the one he fired them at." Ryan smiled crookedly. "The man has a mind like a steel trap. No wonder he's so good at what he does."

Hope lifted Celia's spirits. "I'm praying for both of them."

Finn was curled up on her sofa with the cup of peppermint tea her mother had left for her on the table. The sun had already settled below the horizon, igniting the center of the clouds with gold threads and outlining them in deep purple. Finn put her head back and soaked up the sight. As tired as she was, it was such a relief finally to be home.

There was a quiet rap on the door, and she wondered if her mother, who hadn't fussed this much over her in years, had decided to see if she needed some honey for her tea or an extra pillow for her head.

Then, the door opened and John came in.

"Don't get up," he said quickly, seeing her start to push herself off the sofa.

"John!" Finn breathed his name in astonishment, her gaze immediately falling on the prosthesis he was wearing.

* * *

It had been something he'd been working on for almost a month. Amazing the freedom he already had just by bowing to technology. And overcoming his fears.

"Watch this." He walked over to the table, picked up a book and handed it to her.

Finn started to cry.

"Hey." John sat down next to her and lifted her chin until she was looking directly into his eyes. "You don't like this book?"

"I thought you weren't coming," Finn sniffed, searching for a tissue.

"I met a friend of yours while you were in the hospital," John said.

"Who?" Finn tilted her head curiously.

"The Lord."

Finn's eyes searched his in wonder, looking for the truth. And there it was.

"I did quite a thorough investigation," John said. "Would you like to hear my final conclusion?"

She nodded mutely.

"Let me see, 'For God so loved the world that He gave His only begotten son, that whoever believes in Him…'"

"'…should not perish," Finn murmured helpfully.

"Thank you. '…should not perish but have eternal life,'" John finished. "After your accident, I was so angry. I couldn't believe you had put your life in jeopardy for that Calhoun kid, but Ryan said that you lived your faith. He was right. I thought you were the misguided one. The weak one. But that was me, Finn, not you. Ryan said we all have to walk through the fire at some point in our lives and it either takes us into God's arms or away from Him. I thought He had abandoned me in that fire ten years ago and I didn't want anything to do with Him. But, I'm not so thick-headed that I can't look at everything that's happened and see His hand in it. I began to see how He never abandoned me.'' *And He brought me back to you.*

''I think this is the best birthday gift I've ever gotten.'' Finn smiled tremulously.

''I have another one, although, as gifts go, it's not wrapped very well,'' John said. He waited another heartbeat. ''I love you, Finn Kelly, and even though I could probably limp through life without you, I don't even want to try. I want you by my side as long as we live on this earth. You are the most beautiful, courageous woman I have ever met and I want you to be my wife.''

For a moment, Finn was silent as she absorbed the wonder of the things he'd just told her. Then she moved into his arms and leaned against him. ''I love you, too,'' she whispered. ''And I want to marry you.''

''Soon.''

At the slightly ragged tone in his voice, she chuckled against his shoulder. ''Soon,'' she agreed.

He leaned back and pulled a small velvet box from his pocket. ''This is for you.''

Finn's eyes widened. ''You bought me a ring?''

''Proposals, rings, they usually go together, don't they?'' John teased, his eyes lit with emotion. ''It's not a typical engagement ring,'' he warned as she started to lift the lid. ''If you don't like it, you can pick out something else and—''

He didn't finish the sentence because Finn gasped. Nestled in black velvet was a ruby cut in the shape of a heart.

''It's beautiful.''

"If you'd rather have a diamond..."

"No." Finn shook her head as she turned the ring over in her hand and saw an inscription engraved on the inside. *Isaiah 43: 1-3.* One by one, the words of the verse blossomed in her heart.

"I wanted us to have a symbol of the fire," John said quietly. "And a reminder that God keeps His promises—doesn't He."

As he slipped the ring on her finger, Finn closed her eyes and smiled.

Yes, God always keeps His promises.

* * * * *

Dear Reader,

I am so excited to be able to share my first book, *Tested by Fire*, with you. John Gabriel and Finn Kelly worked their way into my heart, and I hope they worked their way into yours. Police officers are expected to deal with extremely difficult—and sometimes violent—situations that can test their faith and chip away at their sense of hope. Like Finn, they have to strike a balance between being professional and compassionate. Not an easy thing to do.

If it sounds like I have I have a soft spot for police officers, it's probably because I'm married to one! I've worried about him, prayed for him and watched the clock when he's late coming home—but I know that he's where God wants him to be and doing exactly what God wants him to do.

I hope we can meet again in the pages of another book, and just watch—I'll probably sneak in another police officer or two, just because I can't help myself!

Blessings,

Kathryn Springer

Love Inspired

EVERLASTING LOVE

BY

VALERIE HANSEN

Camp director James Harris reluctantly agreed to let animal therapist Megan White test her program with his troubled kids. But when Megan's young sister and one of the teens disappeared, all James's doubts and anger rose to the surface, and he railed at heaven. Would Megan's strong faith be able to help James regain his...and win his heart?

Don't miss

EVERLASTING LOVE

On sale September 2004

Available at your favorite retail outlet.

Love Inspired®

A HEART'S REFUGE

BY

CAROLYNE AARSEN

Rick Ethier couldn't refuse his grandfather's
proposition: revive a faltering magazine and be free
to pursue his own interests. The only obstacle was
Becky Ellison, current editor—not a fan of Rick's since
his negative review of her first book. Yet the restless
Rick soon learned that the things he'd been longing
for all his life—love, community, faith—were within
his grasp…with Becky.

Don't miss

A HEART'S REFUGE
On sale September 2004

Available at your favorite retail outlet.

Take 2 inspirational love stories FREE!

PLUS get a FREE surprise gift!

Mail to Steeple Hill Reader Service™

In U.S.
3010 Walden Ave.
P.O. Box 1867
Buffalo, NY 14240-1867

In Canada
P.O. Box 609
Fort Erie, Ontario
L2A 5X3

YES! Please send me 2 free Love Inspired® novels and my free surprise gift. After receiving them, if I don't wish to receive anymore, I can return the shipping statement marked cancel. If I don't cancel, I will receive 4 brand-new novels every month, before they're available in stores! Bill me at the low price of $4.24 each in the U.S. and $4.74 each in Canada, plus 25¢ shipping and handling and applicable sales tax, if any*. That's the complete price and a savings of over 10% off the cover prices—quite a bargain! I understand that accepting the books and gift places me under no obligation ever to buy any books. I can always return a shipment and cancel at any time. Even if I never buy another book from Steeple Hill, the 2 free books and the surprise gift are mine to keep forever.

113 IDN DZ9M
313 IDN DZ9N

Name	(PLEASE PRINT)
Address	Apt. No.
City	State/Prov. Zip/Postal Code

Not valid to current Love Inspired® subscribers.

Want to try two free books from another series?
Call 1-800-873-8635 or visit www.morefreebooks.com.

* Terms and prices are subject to change without notice. Sales tax applicable in New York. Canadian residents will be charged applicable provincial taxes and GST. All orders subject to approval. Offer limited to one per household.

® are registered trademarks owned and used by the trademark owner and or its licensee.

INTLI04R   ©2004 Steeple Hill